Laughter
Tears
and
Some things to think
about

By
John Gent

A RedPen Publication
Copyright © 2011 John Gent
ISBN 978-0-9560870-2-7
www.thejohngent.co.uk

A work of fiction
Printed by Imprint – Church Street Mansfield
Cover design John Gent

This compilation of short stories and poems is the result of fourteen years of putting pen to paper – often delving into my innermost thoughts and memories for inspiration. I make no apologies for the down to earth subject matter or the many threads of Spirituality that are present – I consider that my sixty-seven years of living a working-class life on this World gone mad give me the right to express my own opinions in my own way.

This book is dedicated to my wife, family and friends who supported me throughout the long, very long, period of 'finding myself'. I sincerely hope that you will 'find yourself' one day...it could change your life...it changed mine.

You may also like to read my other books:

Ties that Bind

The Loop

Contents: Short Stories

CONTENTS: POEMS

Aphrodite's Rock

"Don't pack me any swimming trunks, I'm going au naturel." Jason paraded around the bedroom, thrusting his stuff like a Mr Adonis competitor on heat.

Donna watched the demonstration of 'how to look silly with no clothes on', shook her head, and continued with the packing.

"Them Greeks can get ready; here I come." Jason flexed his biceps.

"Cypriots darling…and be careful how you swing around, you nearly knocked the vase over. Will three pairs of shoes and the Nikes be enough for you?"

"Plenty. Don't forget my favourite Man U shirt, the short sleeved black one."

"Would you still marry me if I did?"

"Only if Jordon was busy that day." Another twirl threatened the cat, the feline hissed as the appendage danced near her nose.

"Swine; a woman is more than a pair of boobs; we do have other benefits you know."

"Come here and show me yours." He lunged for her, slipped on the polished wooden floor and ended up on his back, a breathless imitation of a prize, tiger skin rug…tail and all.

Donna laughed. "Now then…I could take advantage of you if I wanted too…dominate and abuse your body. I could, but you'd enjoy that far too much; sexist pig. Get yourself up and help me to close this case."

Two cases packed, locked and labelled, all was ready for their dream wedding and honeymoon.

Well…Nearly everything.

"Donna, I know it's a woman's prerogative to lie about her

age, but you are twenty-one aren't you?"

"Why?"

"Well, if you're not, we are in deep trouble."

"How come?"

"I'm looking at these papers from the travel agent's. It says here that for a wedding in Cyprus, the bride and groom must be over twenty-one, if not, they must have parental consent. Something about a Statutory Declaration form that must be stamped and signed by a solicitor."

"Bugger."

"I take that as a no."

"Well, I'm nearly twenty-one; in July; the tenth actually."

"Donna, nearly, is not good enough. You either are, or not...simple as that. It's like saying to the Crematorium people, *'my mum's nearly dead; the doctors say she's only got a few weeks left, but can you please burn her now because it's more convenient.'*"

"You don't like my mum, and she thinks you're cute. She'll see another side to you now."

"Donna, you're missing the point; I do like your mum; I'm simply trying to emphasise that nearly is no good. Twenty-one is good, nearly twenty-one is not."

"We paid all that money to Thomson's; they should have sorted this out." Head in her hands, she squatted next to the case. "We fly in two days, what can we do?"

"I don't know. Tell you what, I'll look on the internet, Ask Jeeves may help." Jason fired up the computer.

"Good old Jeevesey; you're a lifesaver." He kissed the monitor screen. "The answer is really simple. We just have to ask your Mum and Dad to sign the necessary legal document in front of a solicitor. It's just a formality to confirm that they have no objections to their precious daughter getting married; they can do it tomorrow. Sorted...end of problem."

"If I told Mum that you wanted to cremate her, she wouldn't sign; I know she wouldn't."

"Donna! Oh forget it." Jason realised that he had a lot to learn about his beautiful bed partner; whirlwind romances did have their pitfalls.

*****

The Six Palms Hotel was a real class act. Donna's friend, Judy, had highly recommended it. She'd stayed there two years ago – as part of her wedding package – and was more than satisfied by the care and attention they'd received. The hotel was in Coral Bay, just outside of Paphos; an ideal base for touring the attractions of the area.

Aphrodite's Rock was just a few miles to the east; a picturesque landmark steeped in history and abundant romantic implications. It had recently blossomed as a prestigious wedding venue; May and June were ideal…dry and very sunny without the intense heat of July and August.

An ideal time, an ideal place, and an ideal couple. Jason and Donna had only been together for a short time – less than a year – but long enough to know that they loved each other.

She put up with his silly football obsession – Manchester United came before everything – except sex…of course – and he put up with her designer label brainwashing. They reached a compromise; he agreed to watch the football on the portable TV in the bedroom, and she agreed to buy the Designer clothes only if she liked them.

"What a load of rubbish, a five-star Hotel and no S ky programmes on t he telly in our room. All the channels are foreign; I can't understand a word they say." Jason switched the TV off in disgust.

Donna wasn't too chuffed either…discovering that the big plasma TV in the lounge was the only set able to receive Sky Sports. This meant that on the Saturday, Jason would have to watch the Arsenal/Man U match downstairs; not exactly an ideal situation on their wedding night.

*****

"Do you, Jason, Henry, Warren, take Donna, Mary, Brunt, to be your lawful wedded wife?" Registrar Macronnis asked the nervous groom who was sweating like he'd just completed a marathon. Jason's suit didn't help – a last minute Cypriot substitute for the original Moss Bros ensemble lost in transit. The Amalthus Airways rep, Maria-Helena Pappadoppolis, had apologised with a machine-gunning of broken English, raised arms and a fluttering of her substantial eyelashes.

Jason couldn't fasten any of the coat buttons; much too risky, anyone in range could have been seriously injured whenever Jason had to take in an extra deep breath. The hat would have looked great at Royal Ascot…on a horse.

"I do," he managed to say…eyes fixed on the lovely Donna.

Resplendent in white, and a vision of light and beauty, she would have been a serious contender for 'Bride of the Year'. OK…the dress may have cost £2000, the shoes £400 and the dazzling tiara another bundle of money, so what? In Jason's eyes, she was worth every penny. To stand together, beneath the clear blue cloudless sky, the only sound the gentle lapping of the waves on the warm sandy beach, was priceless. In Jason's eyes, Donna was a Princess. How appropriate, how significant, that they now stood at the very spot where Aphrodite, the Goddess of love, had once walked.

"I do," answered Donna, completing the ceremony. She scooped the veil over the tiara, licked her lips and devoured her husband with her eyes. "Darling…What time does the football start?"

"I'm sure it will be repeated tomorrow." Jason kissed the new Mrs Warren.

A day in the City

WPC 644 Dolores Brownlow stopped in her tracks. A tall, dark-haired, heavily set man stood in her path. 'Middle-aged, white male' would be entered in her report. He'd just appeared, literally. One minute she had a clear view of the entrance to Woolworths, the next, this unusual looking chap was in her face.

"Can you tell me the time please? My gigamatic seems to have a problem in the correlations."

"Almost 10.35, Sir," she replied in her friendly, but official, manner.

"*Almost 10.35?*" The stranger gave the young, blonde woman wearing some type of 20th Century uniform a quizzical look. "I can't put, *almost10.35*, into my gigamatic. Nod your head when it is precisely 10.35 and I will reboot the phaser synch."

Just my luck, she thought – shaking her head slowly – a weirdo.

She pulled the Motorola intercom from the waist holster and discretely pressed the 'Back-up requested' button. "Shit…no confirmation beep," she muttered between clenched teeth, "I knew I should have charged the battery last night."

She decided to stop the first normal looking pedestrian and ask for assistance.

"I do not believe it; I should be asking you for help, not the other way around; why do you think I pay my council tax? This country's gone to the dogs." A man with a serious attitude problem replied. He'd only just escaped the morning scrimmage in Bond Street and was still in tube shock. A veteran of Dunkirk, he'd experienced shell shock on many an occasion, but his recent battle with the infamous London Underground Railway System came a close second.

"I give up," she spluttered. "I should have phoned in sick. My horoscope predicted a bad day for Virgo's."

"Did you nod y our head?" The man with the gigamatic asked. He'd been observing the woman's mannerism's and concluded that she was a perfect match for the stereotype image recorded in his log; 'less than average intelligence, physically attractive, nice legs, slim build, blonde hair and big bosoms'.

"And who the hell are you?" The Dunkirk veteran turned his attention to the spandex enveloped escapee in front of him. "It's a bit early for a fancy dress party, even in this crazy city."

"I'm Captain James T Kirk, Master of the Starship Enterprise, searching the galaxies for new life. And what do I find? A dumb-blonde and a bald-headed emaciated old man with a poor excuse for a moustache."

"Less of the old man, if you don't mind, you master of the queers. I'll have you know that there's plenty of life left in me; thank you very much. I survived six years of muck and bullets to make a better place for the likes of you milad. And – may I tell you – this is not a m oustache but a rare fungus I caught from giving mouth to mouth resuscitation to Engelbert – Mrs. Worbouys pet hedgehog."

"Beam me up Scotty," Kirk dodged the old man's assault with an umbrella.

"And take the village idiot with you," the dumb-blonde screamed.

Cartouche

"Hey! You with the tash; can't you read?"

Brendon took his hand off the ornate wooden door lever and turned his attention to the loud intrusion from behind. "Are you talking to me?"

"Yes sir, I am. Can I ask you to please respect the 'No entry' sign and continue on y our tour?" Security guard Humphrey Doulton pursed his thin lips. Hands clasped firmly behind his back, he planted his size twelve boots within two yards of Brendon's size eights, then slowly swung his right hand in a smooth arc. "The path is clearly marked. Thank you; have a nice day."

Brendon shrugged and smiled. "Sorry." He sheepishly backed away from the locked door. Next time, he decided, he'd bring Laura.

*****

"What do I have to do?" Laura placed a finger on her lips, unsure of what her brother was asking of her.

"It's easy...just be yourself." Brendon went on to explain. "When I give you the nod, take the camera out of your handbag–"

"Which one? The red Fiorelli you got me last Christmas, or the black Radley I bought with my bingo win?" Her pale green eyes focussed on her brother.

"For God's sake Laura, it's not a fashion contest; you're not on the pull either. Listen...tomorrow I want you to distract this security man whilst I get into this certain room at Broomstead Priory."

"Is he young and good looking?"

"Sis, all I'm asking you to do is take this digital camera out of your bag – Fiorelli or Radley, whichever, I don't mind – then pretend that you need help to take a photo in the 'Green Room'."

"Pretend." Her eyes opened wider. "I won't have to pretend; I don't like them new fangled digi things; much too tekky for the likes of me."

"You have no problems sending text messages."

"That's different."

"Well...Whatever...Look, sis, help me with this, and I'll buy you a new bag."

"I've seen a red one I like."

"You've got a deal."

*****

"Now."

Laura instantly responded to her brother's signal.

Everything worked out better than Brendon had planned. The last thing he heard before picking the lock – a skill learnt during a brief friendship with Jed Bradley, the neighbourhood thief – was a tearful, "Now I've broken a nail," from Laura.

Humphrey Doulton – transformed from 'Mister Nasty' to 'Knight in shining armour' by Laura's helpless little girl act – was too busy with the dippy blonde woman with big eyes and enormous boobs, to notice the 'tash man' slip into the 'out of bounds' room.

"Wow...Wow." Brendan whispered, taking his first physical look at the interior of the locked room. White, white and yet more white invaded his vision. Floor, ceiling, the wall in front, even the walls to either side, all were the purest of white...like he'd entered a giant snow ball.

*****

It had all started the night following his first visit to Broomstead Priory, an ancestral home set in beautiful grounds, only a short

8

drive from Brendan's family home. The recurring dream invaded his sleep for the next month. Every night, he imagined himself walking through the corridors of the Priory. He'd look at the impressive rows of statues. Marble effigies of god's and heroes stared back at him. Paintings of beautiful women and handsome men, all dressed in opulent costumes, hung majestically to either side of the pathway.

Then he'd be in the Green Room, standing before the locked door with the '*no entry*' sign.

Nothing ever happened. He'd wake up, restless, wondering why this room was kept locked.

Why did he constantly dream of this room? and what secrets did it hold?

*****

As if impelled by a hidden force, Brendon's body twisted through one hundred and eighty degrees. Facing him was a white door with an oblong plaque pinned in the centre. The size of a serving plate, it was blood-red.

Lifelike images, a b ird, a sn ake, a sc arab – all intricately sculptured – met his gaze.

Of course; he now recognised it as a 'Cartouche'; like the ones in ancient Egypt; like those shown in the Tutankhamun programme he'd watched on the National Geographic Channel.

Placing his fingers on the head of the hawk like figure, he carefully traced each contour of the wings. A tingling vibration shot up h is arm; before he had time to react, Brendan's hands faded away before his eyes. His brain told him to shout 'help' but the words never left his mouth. Seconds later, his entire body melted into the Cartouche.

"Welcome, Master; you have come to rule us."

Brendon gaped at the woman kneeling at his feet.

"The queen spoke of your imminent arrival; she commanded us to stay by the throne. The vigil is ended. Praise to the gods."

"Where am I? And who is this queen you speak of?" Brendon rubbed his hands down the arms of his chair. Precious stones passed by his fingertips; embedded in the yellowest of gold, they sparkled like the stars in the night.

"Queen Nephinia will join us presently. Alceney ran to the royal quarters as soon as your fingers appeared. Only the queen can give you the answers you seek. So it is written. So it must be."

No sooner said, Nephinia rushed into the Chamber of Kings; a glittering, bejewelled gown draped behind her.

"Promised one, you are embodied again; the gods have answered my prayers." She threw herself at Brendon, almost knocking him over. Wrapping her arms around his head, she smothered him in kisses.

"Now that's what I call a welcome." Face tingling from the caresses, he reluctantly pulled away from the most beautiful woman he had ever seen.

Dark blue eyes – made even prettier with the tears – glowed with the brightness of hope. "Prepare the Ceremonial Bath. We must follow the instructions as given to the High Priest."

Brendon followed the queen and her two servants.

Everywhere he looked, ancient symbols stared back at him. He reasoned that this strange place had to be in the Middle East; Persia, or more likely Egypt.

"In a short while, we will take on our duties. The gods have decreed a two day feast in celebration of your Second Coming." Nephinia rubbed a red amulet hanging around her slender neck.

A large statue of Anubis stood to either side of the entrance; the queen lay prostrate before them. Homage over, she stood, kissed each of the jackal headed gods feet, and offered her hand to Brendon. "Come, all is prepared."

A wondrous scent filled the room. Brendon recognised lavender, rosemary and thyme, but there were many other herbs and spices blended into the heady bouquet.

An oblong bath – big enough for at least four people – was sunk into the marbled floor; pink and white rose petals floated on the water.

Nephinia looked at Brendon. "You must immerse yourself for the ordained time. If you rise from the Bath of Life, you will be accepted as my husband, King Ahkmosin the third. Together we will rule the land of the three gods. So it is written. So it will be."

"Hang on a minute." He scratched his head. "Did I hear you correctly? I thought that you said. '*If you rise from the Bath of Life.*' Please correct me if I'm wrong."

"That is exactly what I said. The phial of sand will be upturned on your entry into the bath. If you survive until the last grain has passed to the bottom, you will have fulfilled the prophecy. Leave before this time and the Temple Guard have instructions to kill you as an unworthy imposter sent by the enemies of our faith."

Scratching his head even harder, Brendon decided there was more to this than meets the eye. He took a closer look at the bath. "What are those long black things squirming along the bottom?"

"The serpents of life...or death if you fail." The smile left Nephinia's face.

"Hmm, this is a very difficult choice; can I phone a friend?"

"You speak in riddles; enough, you must decide now." She beckoned the Temple Guard.

Brendon rushed out of the room – he had to get back to The Chamber of Kings...that's where it all started.

He ran up to the golden throne. A sigh of relief left his trembling body; there, in the middle of the chair's back panel, was a blood-red Cartouche.

The Captain of the Temple Guard could only watch as the

imposter vanished into the Throne of Kings.

*****

"Mr Doulton...will you take a picture of Laura and me please? *Outside* of the locked room, if you don't mind."

"Not at all." Mister Nice Guy smiled. "I'm so glad that you now understand why the room is kept locked." He winked.

Disastrous Journey

Diane gently shook her husband. He wasn't asleep; of course not. "John," she whispered in his ear, "Our flight is now boarding…wake up."

"At last," he sighed, "another five minutes and I would have been in Noddyland."

"Another five minutes and you would have been arrested; all the noise you were making." Diane gave her husband a knowing look, took a deep breath and tutted as she gathered the in flight baggage together. Satisfied, she methodically checked the boarding passes and passports were still safe and sound in the black leather handbag she'd bought from the Oxfam shop only last week. "Can't be too careful; not these days," she said to John, who was studying the queues forming at gate six.

The embarking went smooth enough. Yet again, John moaned about choosing the wrong line to follow. He seemed to have a knack for it; give him ten checkout queues in Tesco and he'd choose the slowest; bless him. The problems started with the seating arrangements. John – a typical right side of the brain person – assumed that his seat, 14C, would be next to Diane's 14D. WRONG. On Flight TH44B – a Boeing 747 – an aisle separated them.

Adding insult to injury, seats 14A and 14B were occupied by a large lady and a young boy. The boy sat next to the window. Ingrid – the large lady – was in the middle, next to John.

Describing her as large is being kind to the woman; her backside projected so far from her body that John could have used it as a dining table. Her compulsive talking made John consider hiring a hit man. She rattled on a nd on about the limitations of her ex-boyfriend. "Twice a day's no good to me…the wimp," she'd said with a flutter of her eyelashes.

By the time they reached cruising height, John was losing the will to live. Noting that Ingrid, the sex starved hippo, was busy attending to junior's tantrums, he whispered across the aisle, "I can't stand any more of this, Diane…will you swop seats?"

Out of the frying pan and into the furnace. What a bad trade it turned out to be. The headphones didn't work, and Ingrid the Arse, had been exchanged for Molly the Boobs. There was no way she'd be able to eat anything during the flight…her breasts literally rested on the back of the seat in front. When she reclined her backrest her bosom looked like a pair of trident missiles, armed and ready to launch.

Actually, it wasn't too bad. John – chivalrous as ever – offering to pass Molly her food from the tray. She returned the kindness by letting him use her headphone socket…much preferring to read.

The intercom pinged. "This is your Captain speaking. We are entering an area of extreme turbulence; seatbelts must be worn until further notice." Ping.

John didn't do turbulence. He didn't like fairground rides, adventure parks or anything that shook his head about. Diagnosed with an inner ear problem as a ch ild, he wasn't comfortable with the atmospheric changes incurred during any flight. There wasn't a cure…unless you could do a Worzel Gummage routine and change heads. He had to sit and suffer the nausea and fear as it rapidly engulfed him, hoping it would quickly recede. If not, it would eventually transform into the unmentionable…the 'panic attack'.

"Here, take a tablet now, before it gets bad," Diane passed John a Lorazapam; a smile and a mimed, "You'll be alright," offered as support.

They held hands across the aisle. Onlookers probably smiled, thinking how nice it was that pensioners could still be romantic and openly show their affection in public. But they couldn't see John's ashen face or the sweat dripping profusely into the tissue clutched in his hand, or feel the pressure applied on Diane's delicate hand. No…if so, they would have realised that they were actually witnessing a battle, a desperate fight of mind over matter; of facing the fear, an invisible opponent as real and intense as any physical enemy.

The combination of the tablet, the much practiced, slow and controlled breathing, and the warm, encouraging hand of his wife, worked…this time.

John remained the right side of the emotional on off switch until they landed safely at Puerto Plata airport. Then things took a turn for the worse.

"Due to the escalating storms surrounding the area, and the approach of Hurricane Andrew, we have been instructed by Head Office to send Flight TH44B and all its passengers back to the UK as soon as possible. Please collect your meal voucher from the Thomson's rep at the entrance to the cafe. The monitors will keep you informed of further details." A tall and official looking gentleman with a B ob Marley appearance, instructed the noisy crowd in immigration.

A few hours later, approaching row 14, Diane took her husband's trembling hand. "Right, John, the choice is yours…Would you like to sit next to Molly or Ingrid?"

His bleary eyes sparkled. "Hmm…I'm hoping that the few tots of rum will help me to sleep on the way back…if I have a funny turn you can pass me a tablet. Anyway…I'll sit next to Molly. If it turns rough again, I'd sooner be buffeted by her bosoms than Ingrid's arse."

"Men." Diane rolled her eyes.

First day at school: One.

Little girl.

"I don't like my Mum anymore. She said that I was a big girl now and made me go to that horrid school. And I cried. Proper tears. Not like the ones when it's bedtime and I want to play at nurses with my little brother Jack. He needs a nurse ever so bad, he's only six months old and can't wipe his bum or feed himself. So I help mum with the cotton buds, and pass her the baby lotion with a picture of Jack on it.

I want to stay little and play with Dora the explorer and watch Balamory.

Why do I have to go? Mummy says that I'm ever so clever; I can do all my Bob the builder jigsaws. I even help to make cakes. We made chocolate cornflake ones; Dad said they were yummy; he ate four of them...greedy mester.

I sat next to Sharon something. I was crying so loud I didn't hear her second name.

Mrs Yeomans – the class teacher – said, 'Abi if you stop crying you can have an apple'.

"I don't like apples," I snuffled. She wiped away my tears with her lovely handkerchief that smelled like flowers.

Megan – the little girl with lots of teeth who sat opposite me – tried to help me to draw a cat. But I'm always drawing our Daisy – she's Siamese you know – so I pushed her hand away and told her to leave me alone.

When it was time to go home, I ran to my mummy and told her that I didn't have to go to school anymore because I already knew how to draw cats. She smiled."

First day at school: Two.

Mummy.

"It breaks your heart; your child's first day at school. I know that it happens to everyone, but it's never any easier. Abi has always been clingy; more than most four year olds. I know that's my fault; I spoil her rotten. Can you blame me? The midwife said that she'd never known such a difficult home birth; she didn't agree with having your first baby at home.

There'd been complications from the minute she was conceived. I don't recommend trying to start a family in the back seat of a Toyota Yaris. Them Japanese people must be extremely flexible. John, my husband, would try for a baby anywhere. Randy bugger.

Midwife Sharon had a right ta ta. You see, the cord was wrapped around Abi's neck like a boa constrictor. Poor little mite, she only weighed 5lb 6oz, and that went down at least a pound after she produced the loudest trump I'd ever heard. As God is my judge, we thought an elephant had joined us. For an encore, she parted with the blackest, stickiest gunge you ever did see. It should have been marked toxic waste and disposed of accordingly. 'Where did that come from', I asked? I thought I'd given birth to an alien.

I knew I was in trouble when Abi said to her dad, 'I don't like you. I want my mummy.' Now John is a good husband and father. Not the best cook or washer upper mind you, but he loved Abi to pieces. As much as he tried, Abi was having none of it. It may have helped if he had 42-inch bosoms full of milk, but we will never know.

So, first day at school, I was expecting the worse. I had pre-warned Mrs Yeomans that she should prepare herself, but the tantrum Abi performed was worthy of an Oscar.

I came home crying my eyes out. Later on, after a cup of tea, I phoned John; told him that he could have the pleasure of taking his daughter to School from now on.

He didn't answer.

Fools Rush In

"Are you sure this is the right place? It looks deserted." Rachel wiped the veil of cobwebs from the small doorway.

"You told me to turn left at the last junction. I thought it looked dodgy." Ziggy shook his head.

"Hey, it's not locked. Shall we go in?"

"No. Tell you what…let's stay out here and admire the view. Aren't the brambles and tree stumps pretty? And look over there, hundreds of beautiful pot holes, big and deep. How lovely."

"No need for the sarcasm. I get the picture." She pushed at the door. "Its stuck."

Ziggy gave two good heaves with his shoulder and he was in. "I can't see a thing; you'd better wait here. I'll get a torch from the car."

Rachel watched him traipse back to the car – The Mondeo's headlights exposed the treacherous terrain.

"Good, you still work." He kissed the torch kept for emergencies, slammed the boot lid down, and carefully retraced his steps.

"Remind me to switch the lights off, Rachel. The battery's nearly flat."

The torch beam collected a tumbled concentration of wood, plaster and assorted debris.

"What a shithole." Rachel put a hand to her mouth.

Ziggy's ferreting around was rewarded by the discovery of an oil lamp sat on the remains of a sideboard.

A plate glass mirror had shattered, littering the floor with razor edged shards.

"Pass me your matches, Rachel, we're in luck, it feels like

there's plenty of fuel inside."

"Shine the torch over here then; my handbag isn't luminescent."

The oil lamp's glow unveiled the cabin's interior.

Rachel pointed at the littered floor. "They look like rodent droppings to me. Come on; I'm not stopping here."

"Don't be so hasty." Ziggy's Doc Martin's crunched through the debris. "There might be some hidden treasure amongst all this crap. Here, hold the lamp. I need two hands for this job."

Shouting, "Eureka," he waved a shiny object in the air.

"Well? What is it? It looks like a cheap cross to me."

"Hang about, I'm not sure. Bring that lamp closer. My guess would be silver; it's definitely not gold. What the…? I've just trodden on something."

The skeleton looked like it belonged to a bear or some breed of large dog. The flesh had long since decayed – more likely eaten by the depositors of the droppings. In his clumsiness, Ziggy had broken part of the rib cage.

"If it's a rat I'll throw up." Rachel peeked around Ziggy's shoulder. "What the hell is that?" She aimed a trembling finger at the grisly remains. "That's it; I'm not staying a minute longer." The lamp rattled as she dropped it onto the floor. The flame went out.

"Rachel, you idiot, hang on a minute. Okay, you win, hold my hand, we're getting out of here." He dropped the crucifix and steered her along the trail painted by his torch. On opening the door, an inky-black wall faced them.

"I should have turned the headlights off. I told you to remind me. Damn…we'll have to go back inside. We'll break our necks trying to get back to the car."

"I'm not going back in there."

"OK, and what do you suggest? Tell you what, we could stand here like ticket collectors until daybreak." He manhandled her back into the cabin.

"Hey, Rambo…careful with the coat. You've just made one sleeve a foot longer than the other."

The torch was almost expired; its faint yellow beam reluctant to leave the bulb.

"There it is." Ziggy crept towards the upturned lamp. "Ouch, I've cut my finger."

Kicking the lamp and matches towards Rachel, he squealed, "Do something with that; I'm bleeding to death."

Lamp lit, Rachel put it at Ziggy's side.

He sat on the floor like a giant gnome, watching the plop, plopping of blood into the growing pool.

"If you'd given me the right directions we wouldn't be in this mess. Just look at my finger." He waved it at her.

"Go on…blame me for everything. I bet it's my fault the car battery's knackered. And the mobile…it'll be my fault you've no credit left…again."

"Oh shut up and pass me a plaster. You must have one in that bag of yours. You've everything but a billiard table in there."

"*Please,* would be nice."

"Anyway, clever clogs, you could've brought your mobile."

"My fault again. Here, put your own plaster on." She threw the Elastoplast at his face.

Rachel looked at Mister Tall, Dark and Handsome, putting the plaster on his finger. "*Men,*" she spat, "*why do we bother?*"

He hung the lamp on a hook dangling from the ceiling. "As soon as it's light I'll walk to the nearest village. We'll just have to rough it for a few hours."

"I don't really care what you do." Sat on a rickety stool, she clutched the torch as if her life depended on it; not noticing that the battery had finally died.

"Hey…What was that scratching sound?" Rachel turned her

21

attention to the door.

"I didn't hear a thing. Help me with this mattress I've found in the corner."

"If you think I'm lying on that you're an idiot. Look at the state of it."

"Lie on t he bare floor then; the rats will love you." He dragged the battered mattress into the middle of the room. "That'll do me nicely. Room for another if you're interested." Flashing his teeth like an advert for a toothpaste, he winked.

She ignored the invitation, too busy listening to the increased activity outside. "You must've heard that; it sounded like a wolf." She dropped the torch and ran towards Ziggy.

"Probably just the wind blowing through the trees; I'll go and check it out."

He eased the door open. "I can't see a damn thing; thick as a bloody bag out there."

The dank, rolling mist frightened Rachel.

"There's nothing-" he paused.

"What's the matter?" She rushed to his side.

"Shhh! I can hear something…a heavy breathing sound."

"What is it?"

"Must be some kind of animal; a big animal. Listen…Its more guttural now, and closer!"

He pushed her into the cabin and banged the door shut. "How much fuel is in the lamp?"

"Why? What does that matter?"

"Will you just answer the question?" Spittle dripped off his bottom lip.

"Okay. Okay. Keep your nappy on. Not much."

"It was nearly full when I had it. If you hadn't dropped the bloody thing we'd be alright."

"That's it, blame me again. You make me sick."

"Aw, shut it woman." Sweat trickled down his nose; big,

brown eyes danced around in their sockets. "There's something outside that don't sound too friendly, not enough fuel in the lamp, and another six hours before daylight, so will you please back off...*now*."

"That thing outside; what is it?"

"How do I know? Whatever it is sounds pissed off and angry...it reminds me of you."

"Pig! If you were a real man you'd go and chase it off or something. But as you're not, get over here; we need to push this mattress up to the window." Rachel pulled the false nails off, placed them in the precious coat, then tossed it like a rag onto the sideboard.

They used the broken furniture to barricade the door, then held hands underneath the lamp.

"It's clawing at the door. Jesus ...that smell, it's revolting. Do something, Ziggy. Please do something."

"And what do you suggest? Spray it with deodorant. Why don't you tell it that you've got a headache? That normally does the trick."

"When we get out of here we're finished." She released his hands and took a step back.

"Thanks for the incentive, Rachel. You know, it makes such a difference at times like this."

"Listen… The noise has stopped. Maybe it's run away."

"Well I'm not going outside to find out."

"Ziggy."

"Yeah."

"This door is the only way in, isn't it?"

"I didn't see any other. Why?"

"Well, the scratching noise has moved; it's now coming from that corner over by the fireplace."

He concentrated on the dark area. Nothing moved.

The fearsome sounds grew louder. The scratching quickened

and intensified.

"My God, the wall's moving. Get back Rachel. Go on, move towards the door. It's trying to get in."

A brick eased out of the wall and clattered onto the floor; another one quickly followed. A hairy claw appeared in the opening.

Within seconds, more bricks fell into the room as a second claw joined the first.

Mortar dust flew everywhere. A huge and deformed snout, appeared in the ragged hole.

A feral smell poisoned the air.

More bricks cascaded to the floor.

Hairy, snarling jaws now filled the enlarged aperture. Thick, green slime, dripped from the massive canines.

The walls shuddered as the creature forced its body through the crumbling brickwork.

It was in. A bloodcurdling howl filled the cottage.

*****

The beast was angry. This was her son's final resting place. The man beings were not allowed to use the cottage. They had killed her only child; a single bullet to his heart. They had paid the ultimate price.

The last transgressor – a small man with a broad white collar around his neck – had scurried away at the sound of the first howling; vanishing into the night like a wraith.

She'd heard the car enter the hallowed grounds; watched the man and woman enter the cottage. The smell of fresh blood had whetted her appetite. Tonight she would feast on man flesh. He was big and powerful. A worthy opponent.

'*The fools didn't see me looking through the window. The man has a mate; skulking in the corner like a frightened mouse. She will do for afters. No hurry.*'

*****

The wolf beast stretched its head until the bulbous wet nose almost touched the spellbound Ziggy.

The foul breath made Ziggy cough. "Get outside, Rachel. Try and make it to the car. Run."

He watched the beast transfigure into a two-legged upright stance. Its pointed ears almost touched the roof.

A primeval growl rattled in its throat. Evil, red eyes scanned its prey.

Ziggy threw himself at the beast, landing a few hard punches to the head. But it was a waste of energy…like hitting a stone wall. Sixteen stones of prime, human muscle was pushed around like a tailor's dummy. A lightweight versus a super heavy. The result was inevitable. He accepted his fate, but he had to stall the finale and hopefully give Rachel time to make it to the safety of the Mondeo.

Gritting his teeth, he renewed his attack, putting everything he had into one last attempt at hurting the beast. Sadly, all to no avail. Within seconds, he could barely move his arms to even protect himself from the savage blows as blood oozed from his shredded forearms.

A sickening swipe to the head knocked Ziggy to the floor. A triumphant howl announced the beginning of the end.

The creature straddled the unconscious body.

The beast wins.

A distant, anguished sound dragged Ziggy from the comfort of unconsciousness. Expecting to see the gates to Eternity, he opened his eyes. The sight before him would live in his memory until Judgment Day.

The beast was threshing about…clutching at something in its head. A shiny object, was impaled in its left eye.

Ziggy watched the blood spurting from the wound.

A pitiful yelp replaced the growl. The convulsions stopped.

Claws opened and fell away from the object refusing to leave its eye. The creature staggered, tumbled backwards, legs flailing wildly in the air.

Ziggy struggled to his knees. The writhing animal lay close by…its red tongue undulated with each gasping breath.

The beast dragged its dying body to the middle of the room, as if forcing its way through a sea of glue. A long, shallow intake of air caused a fluttering of its bottom jaw.

Twisting its body over to face the floor, a broken howl rattled in its throat. The eyes closed, the breathing stopped and silence filled the room.

"That'll teach the bitch." Rachel stepped out of the fireplace. Covered in soot, she shook her tangled hair.

"You…you killed the beast." Ziggy looked at her.

"Sure did. Beauty wins again."

"The cross…you used the cross I thought was made of silver."

"Wrong again, Rambo. It was the silver letter opener I always keep in my bag. Aunt Isobel insisted it was a genuine antique. 'Come in handy one day', she said."

Ziggy collapsed onto the mattress. "Room for one more." He mouthed, then fatigue claimed his battered body.

Rachel held the lamp over her gruesome handiwork. "But…it can't be," she spluttered. "It was definitely a w olf." She stared at the naked body of an old woman, lying across a collection of bones, as if caressing them. Aunt Isobel's letter opener stuck out of the corpse's left eye; a final reminder that evil will always be defeated.

The Gardens of Love.

"Brian. Meet me at noon, the usual place, Eleanor."

I played the message back. Yes, it was Eleanor...her velvety voice made my heart race.

9.07am – the answerphone confirmed the time.

"Wow, that was close." I stabbed the delete button. The realisation that my last minute call of nature had imperilled our secret gave me goose bumps. Five minutes earlier my wife Sally would have picked up.

It never should have started. It was Sally's fault. We argued – as usual – over Sally's mum. The final straw was when the obligatory display of tears ended, and she turned on me like a rabid dog.

"Whether you like it or not, she's staying, and that's an end to it." She collapsed into the armchair and switched on the telly.

That was it; I'd had enough. Grabbing the nearest coat, I'd decided to leave. I remember shouting, "I'm going out; don't wait up," as I banged the door behind me. The words still haunt me.

I checked my notebook. Damn...I was due at Mrs Holloway's house at eleven. There was no way I could fit her three Venetian blinds in time for my latest assignation with Eleanor.

A quick intake of my wife's smelling salts – one of a vast array of toiletries and medicines she kept in a b asket by her favourite chair – ignited my brain cells into emergency solution mode. Ten minutes later, I had Mrs Holloway's permission to start the job at ten.

*****

She welcomed me like a long lost brother. Three blinds, four digestive biscuits and two cups of tea later, I took the cheque out of the pensioner's hand and left.

Ten minutes to twelve...I just had time to get to the park.

I looked in the rear-view mirror, patted my hair into some form of style and checked my teeth for any wayward biscuit crumbs.

I opened the packet of Trebor mints kept for such occasions, and popped one into my mouth.

SHOWTIME.

The car park was almost full. My first choice was to park in the darkest corner. I rejected this spot when I saw the bicycle with the broken rear light lying on the floor. Settling on the only place left, I locked up and entered the community gardens.

Silence enfolded me like a w arm blanket. Within a few breaths, I was relaxed and ready to meet my Eleanor.

This had become our special place.

I reminisced over that first night; the night I met her. Angry and petulant over the mother-in-law tiff, I had driven around aimlessly until I found myself in the empty car park. As if by some divine plan, my exit from the car coincided with the lighting display orchestrated by the setting of the Sun. Sleeping photoelectric cells awoke, igniting the dozens of street lamps surrounding the gardens. Tungsten bulbs fired up, the mass of pale red emissions blending with the pastel shades of a glorious sunset. Transfixed, I had stared at the magical rainbow in front of me.

Flopping onto a nearby bench, I'd closed my eyes and absorbed the tranquillity.

Out of nowhere, something landed on my lap; a small dog with big brown eyes.

"Jemima; you hussy; come here," the young, blonde haired woman said, patting her knee. Levelling her blue eyes on me she said, "I'm so sorry; she's not usually as forward as this;

obviously she likes you; my name is Eleanor."

That was how we met, six months ago. Six wonderful, happy but emotionally destructive, months ago.

"Brian."

The voice of my lover brought me back to the present.

She walked, glided towards me; the dog trotted by her side.

My heart raced. She was wearing the new blouse I'd bought for her birthday; everywhere it touched screamed 'hold me'.

Jemima looked from one to the other as we held hands.

My guts twisted into a tight ball. Avoiding Eleanor's eyes, I spoke quickly. "We have to end it...Now. I can't keep up with the lies and deceit any longer."

Before she could respond, a gang of teenagers ran through the entrance. Birds scattered and Jemima barked.

We pulled apart and made an exaggerated fuss of the dog.

The teenagers giggled and ran away.

Eleanor slipped her arms around my neck. "But...you love me, Brian. You've told me a hundred times that you love me. And Jemima...look, she's ever so upset." Tears welled in my lover's eyes.

"Sally's getting suspicious. I caught her ferreting through my suits yesterday. She pretended that she was sorting some things out for the dry cleaners, but the look she gave me said otherwise. If she'd found the 'to the one I love' birthday card you sent me, we'd have been in real trouble. I couldn't have argued that one away; it would have ended with me admitting my guilt; I've never been a good liar." The last few words fragmented. I looked at Eleanor. We were both crying now.

A loud yapping broke the silence. Jemima had squared up to another dog, defending the two people she loved the most.

We looked at Jemima then back at each other. Smiling through the tears, our eyes locked.

"Kiss me," she eased her lips towards mine. "Kiss me." Her

eyes closed.

I couldn't speak, didn't want to speak. To talk would have broken the spell, the connection, the bond. Everything became so...clear. This was why I lied, deceived my wife, risked everything for a few brief periods of togetherness. Oh yes, the daily torment of adultery was horrendous, soul destroying, but the other option was far, far worse.

I loved Eleanor. She made my heart sing. Nothing else mattered.

I kissed her.

Hormones

"Any more lip from you, Sonny Boy, and you're grounded."

"But Mum," Liam pleaded, "it's her fault." He gave his big sister a filthy look. "Lizzie started it."

Elizabeth Henrietta Hutton – Liam's pain in the side and the bane of his young life – stuck her tongue out.

"Look, she's making faces. Tell her to stop it."

"How old are you?" Mrs Hutton waved the rolling pin like a baton.

"Seven...But Mu um."

"Well, act your age then. And just you remember this, babies don't go fishing with their dads."

"Can I go?" Lizzie had the *butter wouldn't melt in my mouth* look at full intensity.

"No you can't. It's bad enough without you joining the fishing brigade. Come here and help me with the baking. Get the spare apron from the sideboard." The busy housewife swung into action. "When you've done that you can prepare the pine table. The bag of flour is already open."

Lizzie crossed her arms, stamped her feet, and threw the Beano comic onto the floor; no longer interested in the source of the latest sibling argument.

"And less of the tantrums, madam." Mum waved the rolling pin under her daughter's nose. "You may be twelve but you're not too big for a slap."

"She's blobbing her tongue out." Liam pulled the frilly edge on his mother's apron.

"Give me a break, will ya. You two will drive me to drink. I'll be glad when you're both back at school. Stop the bickering and do as you're told. Lizzie, move your backside at once...and you, Liam, get yourself out of my sight."

"Can I go outside to Dad?" His face lit up.

"You can go to Mars if you want to…and don't get that shirt mucky."

*****

"Dad."

The shed door was propped open with a broom handle; Dad Hutton sat at the bench.

"Hello trouble." He swivelled around to face his son. "Are *they* giving you a hard time?" Opening his arms, he beckoned Liam to come closer.

"Mum's got it on her...again, and our Lizzie's being a right b.b…bitch."

Mr Huttons's eyebrows stood to attention. "Hmm, that's an...interesting new addition to your vocabulary." He coughed and hid the smile behind his hand. "Listen son, a bit of man-to-man information. The female of the species, they're different to us. Learn this lesson whilst you're young. Hormones…it's them hormones. And another thing whilst I'm at it, remember this, Liam, a shed and a fishing rod are two of man's best friends. Don't let anybody tell you any different."

"Yes Dad. I'll try to remember. Hormones…are they catching?"

"Well...Almost. You don't actually get the disease, you just suffer the effects. You'll find out as you get older."

"Can we go fishing? I'll dig up some worms." Liam made for the door.

"Sorry, not today son, you'll have to wait till Saturday. Be a good lad and pass me the new reel. It's on the shelf behind you; it says 'Shakespeare' on the handle."

"Is this it?" He wasn't sure about the spelling, so he just grabbed the shiniest one.

"Well done lad. I've just bought a hundred metres of twenty

32

pound line. We can't use the five-pounder at Newark."

"Is Newark special Dad?"

"Sure is, son. The river Trent runs through Newark. A mighty river teaming with specimen fish. The barbel and carp are massive."

"Dad...How big is massive?" Eyes the size of footballs, he looked into his father's face; noticed the blue eyes getting brighter, then sparkle like fireworks on bonfire night.

"This, son, is massive." He opened his arms and touched both sides of the shed. "Could be twenty pounds or more of fins and scales fighting for dear life. Man against fish; a battle royal. And the fish often wins. Lives to breed, to grow, to once more play the ancient game of hunter and hunted."

"Liam! LIAM!"

"Better get back, son, the Ayatollah is calling."

They both laughed.

"Do me a favour, son."

"Anything Dad...you only have to ask."

"Now, I know it won't be easy, but can you do your best to keep Mum nice and sweet for a few days. She doesn't like me spending so much time with my fishing. She got really funny with me last Sunday night."

"Hmm...was it because you didn't take us to church? Mum had a right strop on because we had to walk. Lizzie and me struggled to keep pace with her. We thought she was practicing for the Olympics."

"I'm sorry about that Liam, but your mum knew about the meeting to organize the big fishing contest. I had to go; for God's sake, it only happens once a year."

"I heard Mum talking to Father Murphy. Your name was mentioned...and that Charlton Heston chap."

"What? Are you sure?" Dad's eyebrows erupted again.

"Well, as I remember, he played the big, white-haired man in

The Ten Commandments film. I've seen the film twice; it was definitely him who carried the tablets down from the mountain."

"Oh...right. What else was said involving me?"

Liam scratched his head. "Mum went on about you and your fishing and the Holy Father kept talking about the writing on the first stone. Something about you having no other gods before somebody else."

"Is that it?"

"More or less...Our Lizzie kept prodding me in the ribs; I might have missed a bit."

"Good lad, Liam; thanks for telling me. I get the gist of their conversation, so the favour I was talking about is very, very important. For sure...our trip to Newark could depend on it."

Father and son locked eyes.

"Your mother isn't daft, so you'll have to be subtle in your approach. I suggest you start by taking your dirty shoes off before you go into the house. She's always going on about the sludge on the carpet...And don't mention the bitch word, or hormones. Okay?"

Liam wasn't sure what the word 'subtle' actually meant, but he understood the general idea. He left his father working on the Shakespeare and made his way back to the kitchen.

"Mum, I'm here."

"Wipe that silly grin off your face. Go on, help Lizzie to empty the rubbish bin...and no fighting...do you hear? And be quick about it; dinner's nearly ready."

"Guess where I'm going on Saturday?" He had to tell his sister.

Lizzie scowled. "Don't know and don't care."

"I'm going to the big river; me and Dad's going to catch a monster."

"As if I'm bothered; Mummy's taking me to have my ears

34

pierced…so there." Her tongue almost hit Liam in the face.

"Eat my shorts, b.b…bitch."

"Mum. Liam's being rude again."

"That's it, young man; I've had enough; you're grounded. Get up them stairs, NOW!"

"But Mum." He turned on his best sulk and walked away. "Dad was right," he said to the floor. "Hormones."

I Never Did Like Liver

I never did like liver. I blamed Miss Turton; she tried to force feed me the vile stuff when I was in the third year of Junior School.

"Little boys should be seen and not heard," she'd said, waving the fork like a ceremonial sword; enforcing the threat with a look that could turn milk sour.

You see, I had to stay for school dinners because Mum did a cleaning job for Mrs Sansom at The Manor.

Mum used to make her own cream cheese. I can see her now, shaking the clots of milk out of the co-op milk bottle into the muslin cloth stretched over the draining board. 'Waste not want not', was her motto.

Dad's motto was, 'When in Rome do as the Romans do'. He'd never been further than Skeggy so how could he know what the Romans did?

He should have said, 'when in Pinxton do as the Pinxtonians do', but Dad always got it wrong...Mum said so.

'You couldn't pick your nose', she loved to say – usually after Dad had donated another shilling to Knocker West's pension fund. Jimmy West was in my class; his dad was the local bookie who took the sixpence each way and shilling win bets in the Miners Welfare Tap Room.

'You should talk', Dad would answer, 'You must have been drunk when you chose yours'. Then they'd laugh. I loved to hear them laugh.

"Why do they call your dad Knocker?" I asked Jimmy one day, walking home from school.

"Something to do with playing dominoes. He never wins; he's famous for it. He can only enter the single's competitions;

no bugger will have him in the pairs. Mum says so...she's always right." Jimmy answered, wiping his nose first on the back of his right hand, then on the back of the other.

'Bugger'. I remember saying that word in front of Mum: she nearly swallowed the toothbrush. 'Let me hear you say that word again, and I'll shove this here bar of carbolic soap into that filthy mouth of yours'. She'd picked the foul smelling lump off the sink and pressed it onto my lips. Not a nice memory, but it made me watch my language.

The good old days...before the explosion at the pit...Dad was alive then.

Tuesday was 'take Mum shopping day'. She really loved Morrison's and their '2 for 1' offers. She had a cupboard full of tinned food. Princes red salmon and Fray Bentos corned beef were her favourites.

We always finished off with dinner in the restaurant.

"What will you have Mother?" I passed her the menu. "Today's special is liver and onions; I'm having the fish."

I saw a tear roll down his face

I saw a tear roll down his face; I'd never seen my father cry before. I looked away while he brushed the offending cheek with his hand.

"Go down ta coalhouse, son; fire needs mending."

It never did, but I didn't argue, Dad was going through a bad patch…off work with a beat knee. It had to hurt, but he never complained.

I took the battered, old tin bucket off the doorstep and walked the few yards down to the coalhouse. The swollen knee wasn't the real reason for Dad's tears. Something was wrong. Very wrong.

I took my time filling the bucket, carefully placing the shiny lumps of Kenny coal to one side of the heap. Mum only used it on damp mornings when the fire refused to go; a couple of pieces laid on the grate always did the trick. Quick to burn it could explode, firing deadly shards across the hearthrug. Tinker, our cat, had many a near miss.

Mrs Travers, our next door neighbor, said hello as she passed me on her way to the outside lavvy. She never had kids. Albert, her husband, was killed in the pit, many years ago. A methane gas explosion created three widows that Monday morning in June. She didn't have many friends or visitors; a one-eyed tabby cat called Monty was her only companion.

I did a few odd jobs for her…fetching and carrying and such. She wasn't a strong woman. Every other day, I ran to the corner shop for bread and groceries, and on a Saturday, I queued up at Walker's the butchers in the market place. Two pork chops and a pound of brisket would last her all week.

Once a month she'd get the widow's coal allowance. The coal delivery men should've tipped twenty bags inside the coal house but never did; the last few invariably ended up on the floor…idle beggars. Never mind, she always gave me a shilling to clear it up.

I was still killing time messing about with the coal when she came out of the toilet.

"Whats up our Eric? Yer look real off it today, has ya Mam clipped yer one?"

"Not yet…but day's young."

"Can yer do a b it of gardening for me on Sat'day? Mr Murphy's done his back in agen. I'll treat yer."

Connie Travers used the phrase 'treat yer' to disguise the fact that the payment would be discretionary. Anything from a shilling to half a crown, decided by what coins were in her purse at the time. She'd place the money in my hand as if giving me the Crown Jewels, with the advice, 'don't spend it all at once,' delivered with the last coin.

Wacko. I could go to the pictures the next week.

Tarzan was my favourite. A double bill was showing at the Odeon cinema. Seeing Cheetah get up to his silly tricks always made me smile.

I did feel sorry for Mr Murphy…always broke because of his passion for 'the horses'. He lived at the end of our terrace and did odd jobs and gardening for most of the street. Never mind, I'll nip round later and take him one of my special gobstoppers.

I'd messed about enough, time to go back in. I rattled the door latch to give notice I was around.

They were both crying now. Mum fussed about at the sink moving the pots around in the bowl; Dad pretended to have something in his eye, rubbing a hankie across his face to hide his embarrassment.

Coal bucket placed on the hearth, I sat at the kitchen table.

Playing around with a knife and fork, I tried my best to avoid eye contact with the pair of them, especially Dad. I failed.

"Eric."

"Yes Mum."

"Dad's just come back from't Doctors. Dr O'Shea won't sign him off the sick, says he needs another month off work. Club money aint a lot so we'll have to watch our pennies and cut back a bit."

"Mum, you don't have to give me any pocket money this week. Mrs Travers wants me to dig her garden. It's a r ight mess. I might get half a crown if I do a good job."

"Eric...Mum's trying to say we're skint. Rent's due tommorrer and we aint gor it."

"We can lock the doors and hide behind the curtains. Tommy Flint says they do it all the time." I looked at Dad; he'd given up trying to hide his tears.

"It's not just the rent, son. Ya'll have to wait for the bike."

I ran to his side. He held me that close I could hardly breathe. "But Dad, you promised me a n ew one for my birthday." I wriggled away.

"There's always Christmas. Things should've picked up be then."

I wasn't happy. Dad had promised me the bike. He never broke a promise. Never ever. "But Dad I really want one." I was crying now.

"What yer want and what yer get is another matter," Mum barged in. "It wont hurt you to go without a new bike. Snap on't table and a roof over our head's more important. You'll have to manage with the old un."

I sat at the table, sulking. I was too big for the old Brookes Junior. Dad had said as much last month. 'Ya should be riding a Raleigh Hercules, with Derailleur gears. Them Sturmey Archer's are alraight but they've only got three gears. Right old fashioned. Ya''ll be a teenager next birthday. I'll take yer to Currys; ya can pick whatever colour you want. That's a promise son, but ya've got to be a good lad, do what ya mam says. No answerin back, ya hear.' I remembered every word.

I had been a good lad. Never answered back to Mum. Wouldn't dare. Barely five foot in height, she was at least eight foot in attitude. Whenever she had it on her, best look out; even Dad knew his place. I'd seen many a dinner thrown onto the fireback. Any criticism of the meals provided received an immediate and explosive response.

"I'm not yer slave yer know. If you can do better ger on wi it, and clean yer mess up after yer," she'd scream before grabbing the plates off the table and hurling the contents into the flames.

Dad sat next to me, his large hands covering mine.

"It can't be helped son. Ya know I wouldn't let ya down on purpose. It's me knee. Six weeks of sick pay don't go very far. I didn't expect O'Shea to give me a note for another month. By Christmas we'll be OK. Ya'll get yer bike then."

Dad helped me to do up the old Brookes Junior. We lifted the seat, raised the handlebars and oiled the chain and gears; it was a different machine. I missed the Tarzan double feature; the half a crown treat from Connie bought some proper lacquer paint from Woolworths. British Racing Green looked great on the old boneshaker.

Dad returned to work a month after my thirteenth birthday. His mates at Blackwell Colliery had a whip round that made fifteen quid. Dad was right chuffed.

"Salt of the earth, miners," Mam said with a tear in her eye.

I never did get the Raleigh Hercules. Tommy Flint offered to do a straight swop when he saw what Dad and me had achieved with the old Brookie; his Philips racer was always going back to Currys workshop; them Derailleur gears weren't half as reliable as my Sturmeys. The vintage machine did me proud till I finally outgrew it; by then I was an apprentice electrician at Blackwell Colliery.

Three years later, on my eighteenth birthday, I signed a hire-purchase agreement to buy a 250cc Norton Dominator with a full fairing and took my latest girlfriend to Skeggy…but that's another story.

I was only nine years old when Dad walked out

I was only nine years old when Dad walked out.

A white Stetson hung over his face, as if ashamed of its owner.

The last thing I heard him say was, 'Bye Junior. See Yah', as he got into the cab.

Momma always said Dad was OK…a good man. Jack Daniels was the problem.

I grew up hating all three of them. Dad for taking the easy way out, Momma for depriving me of a father, and Jack Daniels…whoever he was.

I soon learnt how to wash dishes, peel the veg and empty the trash. It helped Momma a little…least she said so. She had the eight to four shift at Lucy's Diner. 'Two mouths to feed and rent to find. Did what I could. Needs must,' she always told me.

To this day, I blame Lucy's for most of my problems. 3.30 sharp, straight from East Sixth Street Primary, I'd go into the 'staff only' corner booth, eat my fill of the steak burgers and fries. Fast food. Texan style.

Digestive problems, mobility limitations and the type two diabetes were my long-term inheritance.

I left Austin Secondary in 98, the biggest twelfth grader in school. A five and a half foot lump of lard, tipping the scales at the wrong side of twenty stones.

My friends called me Willie; everyone else called me Blobby.

Momma still worked at Lucy's. The owners had changed a few times, but 'Lucy's' still hung over the entrance. Mrs Rosetta Herandez, the new boss, kept the old blue neon sign, as all the others had. Why change it? the regulars still came in.

Momma was now touching forty…she looked more like fifty. Not really her fault. She did her best. She never had a break, had to pull the weekend shifts to make ends meet.

A friend of Momma's worked in the local WalMart on Jackson Street. Said there was a job stacking shelves if I wanted to apply. What options did I have? My grades were poor and my physical appearance didn't help my prospects one little bit.

My first wage packet was two hundred bucks. Momma said I should keep a hundred, on c ondition that from that day onwards, I would buy my own clothes, and luxuries…like going to the movies and such.

'Try and put a few dollars by, you never know what's coming,' she'd said, ironing the white blouse with Lucy's emblazoned across the front.

I'd been taking the Diabinese tablets for a w hile. Luckily, the health insurance plan came with Momma's job, covering the prescription costs. Possible side effects were mentioned on the back of the packet – small print of course. No wonder I had the gut problems. Visits to the toilet were certainly becoming more frequent, and I farted like a hippo…phewee...Gross City.

It was Donna pushed me into doing something about my obesity – she did check out in the store. She took to me straight away and sympathised with my weight problem. Said her teenage brother, Tyler, had been really massive. Had been...A cardiac scare last year had pushed him into action. They gave him fair warning, the docs at the clinic, 'unless you alter your diet, and lifestyle, you'll never make the forty'.

"Scared him shitless," Donna said.

A year later and he's dropped five stone. Looks good and feels great.

"He exercises every night at Benny's Gym. Limits his food intake to two thousand calories a day; it works." She told me.

Donna…a great gal. I asked if she'd help me with the calorie thing. I'd no idea what to do – numbers weren't exactly my speciality.

Momma was supportive. Stopped buying the chocco bars and banned me from the diner. Surely did; she kick started the new healthy regime. Thanks Momma.

I booked a month's trial membership to Benny's; did my first workout last week. Holy Moses was I shattered. Two minutes on t he treadmill and I shook like a jelly…like three jellies. I never sweated so much in my life. You could hear me gasping for breath from across the street.

I'm way out of condition, and there's a long way to go, but I'm positive about it all. I'm determined to get there…or die trying.

Jacob Martin

"Jacob Martin, please take your farmyard manners out of this classroom…Immediately."

Miss Taylor – the latest student teacher assigned to Mexton Secondary Modern – was disgusted with the belching and farting produced by the large, heavy limbed boy sat on the back row. She'd tried to ignore his appalling antics, but the whispered giggles from Monica Howard, who sat in front of Bunter – the class nickname for fourteen years old Jacob Martin – had suddenly developed into a loud guffaw.

"Move it, young man, or else." Teacher pointed her chalky fingers to the door.

"Jesus Christ, Miss, not again?" Jacob spluttered.

"And wash your mouth out whilst you're at it, the Lord's name will not be spoken in vain in my presence." She threw the chalk at the blasphemer.

He knew the consequences of 'or else'. Only last week he'd upset the same teacher during the humanities' lesson. She'd invited the thirty students to give a two-minute talk about their father's occupation. Jacob had meant to say, 'Dad works down the pit' but the words got corrupted somewhere between his brain and his tongue. Dad works down the *tit* assaulted Miss Taylor's sensitive ears.

It wasn't entirely his fault…Doreen Clarke was as much to blame as he was. She had the biggest boobs in the class and shouldn't have been wearing that shirt with the button missing. The slip of the tongue had earned Jacob a visit to the Headmaster's office.

"The next time you incur a reprimand, *boy.*" Mr Kenneth Stubbs, MBE, attacked Jacob with a look that could melt steel.

"You will be introduced to the appropriate punishment."

Jacob knew that he didn't *fit in*. Most of his classmates ridiculed him, calling him 'Chubby chops' and 'Lard Arse'.

The final insult came after the BBC screening of the 'Billy Bunter'series. Martin Flint shouted, "Move out the way Bunter," as he pushed by Jacob in the corridor outside class-room four. The name was instantly adopted by every pupil at Mexton. Everyone that is, with the exception of Simon Hilson, Jacob's only friend, who had always called him 'Big Boy'.

Simon lived at 67, York Crescent, two doors down from Jacob's bungalow, with his grandparents...Simon's that is, Jacob's grandparents lived abroad, somewhere in Spain; Costa something or the other.

Back to Simon. He was twelve going on thirteen, but big with it. He loved to hang about with Jacob; probably because they shared the same quirky sense of humour and both had an excessive craving for sweet things. It was a question of who could eat a Mars bar the quickest.

They'd go together to see the latest, 'X' rated 'Horror' film at the Empire cinema; always struggling to keep a straight face as they paid the half-price fare on the bus, knowing that a few minutes later they would brazenly ask the ticket woman for a seat in the one and nine's.

Grandpa Hilson didn't like Jacob. "You'll end up like him. Fat and friendless; mark my words. Fourteen years old and as big as a sh it house...smells like one as well. Does he ever wash? *And* he's a funny colour...looks like one of them Japs I fought in Burma." He'd said this with a scowl and a grunt.

The lecture was a waste of time. Jacob and Simon became inseparable. On leaving school, Simon joined his friend in the Coal Industry; both of them given the nod by Jacob's dad who *knew* someone in the Training office at Billington Pit.

*****

"What a load of rubbish!" Jacob nudged his pal. "We can do better than that."

Simon shook his head. "I'm not so sure; they don't half make a slap when they hit the floor."

"Jesus Christ, Simon, it's all a sh am. If it was real they'd have their own monogrammed bandages in casualty." Jacob booed the hooded wrestler leaving the ring. "'The Derbyshire Mangler', my arse." He shoved two, sausage like fingers in the air.

"Hey, 'Killer Kane', your knickers are showing." Jacob laughed out loud.

*****

"How much?"

"Twenty quid each…Provisional. If the fans like us, we can renegotiate." Jacob did his Hiawatha dance.

Simon was quickly sold on the idea. "Mind you…We'll have to go into a strict training schedule."

"Nahh, no need; the past five years qualify as t hat. Okay, maybe we do carry a lot of weight, but we're both as fit as a butcher's dog; we can thank good old Billington Pit for that."

*****

A month later, they walked into the Norton Heath Stadium; Bunter and The Mars Bar Kid…The Human Dustbins.

They did a novelty tag-match challenge, 'Eat it or Beat it'; they went down a bomb.

Memoirs of a South Normanton Shiner

"I hate school. I'm not going tommorra."

"Ya've got to go…everybody has to."

These are my first memories of living, of being in the world, of existing.

I must have been born. I must have progressed through babyhood. I must have staggered through infantile stages of mobility, crawling, and first hesitant steps towards anxious parents. I must have passed the transition from mother's milk to solid food. I must have…but such events, good, bad, or just happenings, are not in my memory bank – the subconscious depository of the life and times of John Gent Junior.

Going to my first school was a trial. I hated it. Why should I spend time with strangers when I could be at home with Mum and my baby brother Geoff?

Mum loved me. I never ever doubted it. This knowledge helped me through the suffering and enforced daily abandonments at the school gates.

Transport in the late forties was primitive and limited. We lived about half a mile from the Infant's School. Sooner than pay the few coppers to Midland General for the bus fare we used Shank's Pony – Derbyshire code for walking.

Mum would push our Geoff in the coach built pram, whilst I reluctantly followed a few yards behind, sulking and spitting at the floor in feeble retaliation.

Dad worked at the Pit…on shifts…Mum said so. I didn't understand Pit or shifts until I was much older, but at five years of age I did understand that Dad got very dirty.

One day I came home from Hamlet Lane Infant's School to find this strange black-skinned man having a bath in the middle of our kitchen. He sat as large as life in the big tin bath that usually hung outside our back door. It was our bath in our house, what was he doing in it? He just sat there, washing the muck off his body with the Palmolive soap Mum used for my twice a week cleansing in the sink.

I ran outside, straight into Mum, nearly knocking our Geoff from her arms.

"That's only your Dad. Don't be silly, get back in." She smiled at me.

The layers of coal dust vanished under the suds, gradually revealing Dad. He gave me the subdued smile I will always remember him by and offered his large hands for me to run into.

I experienced Panda Eyes long before I knew of the existence of Pandas. It took Dad several washes before he was clean enough to be fully recognised.

My big sister Marlene was five years older than me. She'd no time for a little brother. When Mum asked her to take me out for a walk she wouldn't have any of it…made a right fuss.

"He's always getting in the road and crying. Sally Jones don't have to take her brother everywhere she goes. Anyway, he'd sooner stay with our Geoff," Marlene would cautiously say to Mum; a defiant NO would have meant no pocket money and an 'I'm telling your Dad,' threat from Mum.

It wasn't until much later that I understood and sympathised with our Marlene. By then I was fourteen, House Captain, Prefect and Vice Head Boy in the last year of Big School. Our Geoff had just come up from Junior School, and although I loved him as a brother, I didn't want his company when I was playing with my mates and basking in the glory of my seniority; he cramped my style. I fancied a girl called Josie at the time and I didn't want any 'telltales' getting back to Mum.

Sorry Marlene, and you too Geoff…please forgive me.

Dad worked underground at A Winning Colliery; a ripper in

the coal seam known as the Low Main. He wasn't on good money, but many were worse off than us; at least we had a summer holiday every year.

The first holiday I can remember was in 1950 at the Miners Holiday Camp Skegness. I was almost seven.

We caught the coach in the Market Place. Dad hauled the heavy suitcase as best he could, stopping every hundred yards or so for a breather – no trolleys in them days.

Mum carried two shopping bags full of refreshments for the journey. One contained the pop – Corona of cause – Orange, Lemonade and Dandelion and Burdock. The other one held a mixture of cheese and onion and tomato and cucumber sandwiches and five bags of Smiths crisps carefully placed on the top.

Marlene and me followed with our Geoff walking between us…his little legs going ten to the dozen trying to keep up with us. He held our hands for support and gurgled with laughter whenever we swung his feet clear of the floor.

Before we even got to Lincoln, I'd asked Mum 'Are we nearly there?' half a dozen times.

'Give him another sarnie…and I'll have a bag of crisps if you please', Dad gave me one of his biggest smiles.

Memory is fickle. We always glamourise the good things and conveniently forget how painful and disturbing the trials and tribulations of life actually were, but I have never tasted better tomato and cucumber sandwiches, washed down with warm, Dandelion and Burdock pop.

Almost everyone in the holiday camp participated in some sport or activity…just to be involved sort of thing. Me and Dad went in for the three-legged race. We only came fourth but we should have been disqualified; Dad lifted me up and carried me most of the way. But it was all good innocent fun; nobody grumbled.

Dad came nowhere in the Knobbly Knees' contest and our Marlene was right miffed when her school mate, Mary Wright, finished above her in the Junior Holiday Princess competition.

Mum loved the holiday. No cooking or washing up for a week; no going down to the washhouse and toiling all day long over the dolly tub.

First day of the holidays, Dad bought a bucket and spade for Geoff and me and a beach ball for our Marlene. The sea was miles away – probably just a couple of hundreds of yards...remember, I was only six years old at the time. I only paddled in it the once. It was a horrible rusty colour and so cold it took my breath away.

Friday night was the highlight of the holiday: Camp Talent Competition Final. Dad failed to come anywhere in his heat on the Tuesday. He did a trick with his belly muscles that wasn't fully appreciated by the judges. He said next year he'd bring the Indian clubs from his Army days and give a proper demonstration of how to keep fit and supple. Ted Wallace from Shirland won, singing Sunny Boy. His prize was a silver cup and a £5 note.

The following year's holiday was in Wales, a place called Rhyl...another Derbyshire Miners Holiday Camp. But before that I was to have the biggest scare in my life, before or since.

Off My Trolley

"Tell your mother I don't want any more grapes, and you can take them evil smelling flowers out of the room; they give me a headache."

Sonya glared at her dad. "You're giving everybody a headache. The nurses want a medal."

"That makes me feel much better. Tell you what, pull all the wires and tubes out and fetch Matron. Tell her I don't need to be in a private room anymore. You can put me back in Ward 8, next to Smelly Gordon."

Sonya scooped the Arum lilies out of the vase and threw them in the waste bin. "No wonder our Tyrone won't come; he says you've changed…you're not his dad anymore."

"And that little shit can whistle for that Nintendo console he wants for Christmas. He's got no bloody chance." Harold sat up in bed, almost knocking the water jug off the table.

Nurse Askew entered the room. "Time for your tablets… 'Grumpy'." She forced back a smile.

"And you can piss off." Harold picked an apple off the table. "One wrong word from you and I'll shove this right up your arse."

Sonya took the nurse into the corridor. "I'm sorry about Dad. I'm sure he doesn't mean half of what he says."

"Don't think anymore about it. I've heard it all before. 'Isolation' has strange effects on some people. We've had worse cases…I think." Nurse Askew winked at Sonya.

"Mum makes any excuse not to come. She says that if he calls her a 'bag' once more, she'll either kill him or smack him across the face with the divorce papers."

"You have to remember him before the illness…the good times. Try to put yourself in his shoes." The nurse became deadly serious. "You may not know it, but his family history is frightening. The inconclusive X-rays and bad test results must have really frightened your dad.. Then, to top it all off, we shoved him into a private room. '*Solitary*'…that's what some patients call it. I must admit." The nurse moved closer to Sonya. "*I* wouldn't like to be in there on my own…not for the full twenty-four-seven. Imagine, all the time in the world to fret and worry about the pains and how long you must stay in Hospital. I'd go off my trolley…I know I would."

"Our Tyrone's convinced Dad's been taken over by the aliens…you know…like in that 'Invasion of the Body Snatchers' film." Sonya shook her head. "I only hope that you're right, Nurse. If not, you can keep the cantankerous old so and so."

One Good Turn

"Good morning Mister. Nice day for the race."

"What race is that son?"

"The human race." Jimmy flashed a g rin as b ig as t he 'Cheshire cat's' at the man entering the shop.

Bill Smith inwardly reproached himself. A man of forty should know better; that line is older than the hills.

Jimmy was harmless. He worked Mondays and Thursdays in the corner shop; the wages helped to supplement the stingy student's allowance he had to live on.

Bill wasn't stupid or thick, but was very shy. Low self-esteem made him open season for wise cracks, off loading of blame or any emotional shit floating around seeking a target.

This lad's got all of his life before him, lucky bastard, Bill thought to himself. I'd change places any day of the week. Even taking into consideration the multi-coloured mop of hair hanging garland like down the teenager's acne cratered face. Twice his age and not married. Never likely to be either, who'd take to an ugly failure like me? Bill mentally thrashed himself; as per usual.

Bill wasn't ugly, but he had major issues with the huge gap in the middle of his top teeth. A corkscrew twisted incisor at either side of the bottom set, added to his complex. He'd rejected orthodontic treatment as a teenager, and always regretted the decision.

He never smiled, making things worse by frequently talking through the fingers of his left hand.

"Has the Derbyshire Times come yet? I can't see any on the shelf." Bill enquired.

"No, but last week it came just after nine, so it should be here any time now." Jimmy flicked through the current edition of Computer Arts Magazine; he'd read it properly later on, whilst the shop was quiet.

Bill decided to call back later for his weekly intake of the local news. About to leave, a squeal of brakes and the blip on a throttle caught his attention. A Golf GTI had pulled up outside; he recognized the shocking pink hatchback as Alison's car; he'd know it anywhere.

Bill, Algernon, Smith lived at 248, Platt Street, a two roomed upstairs flat. He kept it clean and tidy, helped by the twice-weekly visit cum inspection by his Mum, Mabel.

"I'm sure you used to work for the police forensic team." He once told her. "You could find fingerprints on water."

"Now don't you be coming the sarcasm with me our Algernon." She'd used his, 'Sunday' name, reserved for the rare occasions Mabel Smith decided to admonish her only son.

He could see her now, pulling on the Marigolds and going over the same areas he'd cleaned barely half an hour earlier.

"Filthy; I don't know how you can live in such muck," she'd exclaimed, removing invisible contamination with her magic touch. At least it made her feel better. Her son was a shy loner; unless he pulled his socks up and got out a bit more, he would remain a bachelor.

"Mrs Marshall tells me her youngest has just passed her driving test. It took her three tries mind you…said she had to get her driving licence, a condition of getting promoted to Assistant Sales Manager. Can you remember Alison?" Mrs Smith had sprayed the coffee table with yet another generous coating of Pledge.

"Can I remember Alison? Sure I can." Bill wasn't at all sure, whether Alison would remember ever meeting him, but he certainly knew her.

"She must be about twenty-six now," he'd said, avoiding the latest spurt from the Pledge.

"Thereabouts; I know you're fourteen years older than her because you where in the fourth-year at Frederick Gent's School when her mum went into labour three weeks early. It took us all by surprise…especially Gladys. We lived in Victoria Road then, at number 72; the Marshall's lived at 64. But Gladys and me kept in touch. Alison was still in nappies when we moved to Beech Avenue…Can you remember?"

If Bill could have chosen any woman in the world to share his life it would have been Alison. Not Julia Roberts, Halle Berry or even Demi Moore. No...Alison Marshall would do very nicely, thank you very much.

What his mum didn't know – not many did, unless you were outside the Odeon cinema on the night of Saturday July 7th 2001 – was that Alison Marshall saved Bill Smith from getting his head kicked in by the local bully, Ted Flynn; a well-known trouble seeker who was escorting Alison home from the Angel Pub and disco, next door to the cinema.

Bill enjoyed his Saturday night at the movies. He lacked friends and didn't feel comfortable on his own in pubs.

What actually happened, was Bill accidentally brushed Alison's shoulder as they crossed paths. Ted – out to make an impression on A lison – grossly overreacted and attacked Bill like a rabid wild animal. Throwing Bill like discarded paper to the floor, he'd lined up his size eleven boots to redistribute Bill's brains all over the foyer when Alison stepped in and dragged said boyfriend away.

Ted's show of unnecessary hostility didn't impress Alison, who ditched him as soon as they got home.

"You're a very lucky man." Onlookers had assured Bill as they picked him up. "Thanks to Alison Marshall, you still have a head on your shoulders."

Well I never, saved by Gladys's youngest. It's a small world, Bill remembered thinking as he got up – the only damage being a scuff to his leather coat. Thanks to little Alison – not so little anymore.

He'd glimpsed Alison as he'd fallen; remembering the woman he'd come into contact with was very attractive, with long legs that went on forever as he traversed the shapely limbs on his way to the ground, mere millimeters away from her smooth flesh.

Two years ago? Even so, the incident never left his memory. He'd thought of sending her flowers or chocolates as a token of gratitude, but even this small gesture was outside of his comfort zone.

In the intervening years, Bill did actually see A lison on several occasions. He'd be leaving the Odeon after seeing the latest Hollywood offering, and there she'd be, interlaced with the latest admirer. Not that she ever recognized Bill…he was just another passer-by and invisible.

'Oh Alison…if only.' He'd often thought. Not that he lusted for her. Although that would have been quite understandable since she truly was beautiful. No, it was much more than that. She always looked smart and fashionably dressed in a style that displayed her voluptuous figure without cheapening it, and she never wore too much makeup. And of course…those legs. However, the true 'icing on the cake', was her gentle persona and quietly spoken manner.

Alison was unparalleled in Bill's innocent eyes. Even after leaving The Angel with the usual crowd of Saturday night revelers, she never succumbed to the loud, often lewd mannerisms, like the other girls. Yes, one could certainly have taken her home to see one's mother without any qualms.

A loud sneeze sounded in the shop, dragging Bill back from Memory Land.

"Excuse me, have you any Allereze tablets?" Alison managed to say to Jimmy between the sneezing. She'd been coughing and spluttering all morning and should have bought the antihistamines from Boots yesterday, but forgot. It was getting worse. Tears poured from her turquoise blue eyes, forming train lines through her mascara.

"Sorry, Miss. We don't sell anything like that; we only have Aspirin and Ibuprofen."

Bill observed the activity from behind the magazine rack, torn between a compulsion to assist Alison, and the anchor of shyness and low self-esteem holding him back. As ever, the anchor won.

Alison erupted into a machine-gunning of sneezes then slumped to the floor. She frantically ripped open her handbag, scattering the contents everywhere. "My inhaler, my inhaler," she pleaded. Her hands swept across the polished tiles, desperate to locate the Ventolin spray.

Bill's heart started to race; he couldn't just stand there witnessing Alison's distress without doing something. Rushing to her side, he recognized the small, blue canister at the side of her foot as the same type of breathing relief his mother used when her asthma was bad. Grabbing it, he gave it a vigorous shake before tenderly placing the mouthpiece between Alison's pallid lips.

"Try to relax; I'll look after you," he whispered in her ear as he squeezed the first puff of life into her quivering body. Sitting behind Alison, he supported her head on his chest and squeezed another shot of salbutamol into her gasping mouth. "Don't be frightened; you'll be OK in a minute. My mum suffers with asthma; I've helped her many times. You've just got to keep calm and give the Ventolin time to work." Bill stroked her long blonde hair. Confident he could help her through this trauma, he kept repeating, "you'll be fine…you'll be fine."

Slowly but gradually, her breathing became more controlled, and the body shakes less violent.

Bill turned her face towards his and looked her in the eyes.

"You're doing ever so well, Alison. Take the puffer in your right hand and take two puffs…slowly and as deeply as you can."

Jimmy had kept his head. Realising he was not up to the emergency response the young woman obviously needed, and that the Mister who called for his Derbyshire Times every week seemed to know what he was doing, Jimmy had used his mobile phone to make the 999 call.

When the paramedics arrived, Alison was sitting on a chair that the kind gentleman had made the young lad with the funny hair bring from the store room.

The Ventolin had worked. She now breathed easier; panic mercifully abated. Never did she want to feel like that again. This attack was the worst ever…too close…too frightening.

The paramedics put Alison in the ambulance and attached her to the nebulizer. Fifteen minutes later, they were satisfied that she'd stabilized, but, as a precaution, they would take her to Calow hospital.

Jimmy said, "Hope you'll be OK, Miss," as he passed her the handbag.

"I must thank the Good Samaritan who came to my rescue," she said through the Nebuliser mist. "He saved my life. I'd panicked. Totally lost it. Is he still here?"

"No…He seemed to vanish when the ambulance arrived." Jimmy shrugged his skeletal shoulders.

"Do you know him? Or where he lives?"

"Sorry, Miss…but I can't help you there. You see, he only comes in once a week…on a Thursday…to buy the Derbyshire Times. Very quiet he is…never smiles. But surely…you must know him…I heard him call you Alison."

A vague memory surfaced.

Alison smiled.

One Way Trip

"Shut that effin door before we both fall out. One more trick like that, and I'll do it here." Aldo spat the words in my face.

"Does it matter? I'm as good as dead anyway." I closed the door.

"Stop it…the pair of ya." Gnasher glared at me through the rear view mirror. "Karl, get your act together. You know the score; give the man some slack. And you…Aldo, put that bloody gun away. It might go off."

I looked out of the rear window. The Dog and Hare Inn disappeared in the taillights.

Were they all deaf? I wouldn't have risked Aldo's wrath if I hadn't seen the group of women standing outside. Why hadn't one of them responded to my shout for help? For God's sake, I'd almost touched the fat blonde's fur coat.

Where would this one way trip end? This wasn't the usual area for the…business. Damn, I might not get another chance to escape.

Aldo fidgeted next to me.

"How much further? I need the toilet." His voice quivered.

Gnasher had driven further than I'd expected. That police car at the roundabout must have unnerved him, forcing this detour into the backwoods.

"I'm looking for a suitable spot; shouldn't be far. Tie a knot in it." Gnasher growled.

"That's alright for you to say. Just pull off the road; I'm dying for a piss." Aldo's wriggling got more intense.

Fully expecting to be urinated on at any minute, I inched away.

"What the bloody hell?" Gnasher's voice filled the car.

"Aldo, keep your eyes on Karl whilst I get out of the car. And you, Karl…no more of the Bruce Willis stunts."

Why had we stopped? Was this it?

Through the windscreen, I saw the headlights illuminating a tree trunk obstructing the narrow, country road.

"Aldo, get your body out here; I need a hand."

"Okay Gnasher, but what about action man here?"

"I'll keep an eye on him whilst you get the rope out of the boot."

I assessed the situation. Hmm…perhaps Lady Luck was coming to my assistance.

"Karl…Don't even think about it; you wouldn't get twenty yards before Aldo popped you."

Gnasher must have read my thoughts.

"Go on, make my day. Ya might get lucky…punk." Aldo dropped the rope and waved the pistol inches away from my face."

"Bloody hell, Dirty Harry's joined us. Who'll be next? Effin Rambo. Pass me the gun, *stupid*. Right, now tie him to that tree over there, the big one, three rows in. It'll need both of us to move this soddin thing." Gnasher kicked the lump of wood.

"Why bother? Let's kill him here." Aldo repeated the intimidating gun action.

"Oh yeah, great idea. Less than a quarter mile back they're turning out of the pub. What if they come this way?" Gnasher spat on the ground.

"Sorry Boss…I hadn't thought of that." Aldo slurred.

"That's why Big Errol sent me. Just take Karl over there…like I told you. And shove a hankie in his mouth; we don't want him shouting the odds. Ya never know who might be listening." Gnasher gave the tree another kick.

Aldo steered me towards the chosen tree; the light provided by the overcast Moon just enough to show the way. After a few steps, he slowed down, urgently crossing his legs.

"Bollocks, I need to *go*." He sounded in pain. "And you'd better behave yourself...or else." Aldo struggled to open his fly.

Now, I decided, and ran towards the trees.

*****

Gnasher observed the performance in disbelief. "Aldo, you stupid bastard. Put that...thing in ya hand away and get after him. You'll need a torch; there's one in the boot." He sat on the tree trunk and lit a cigarette.

"Right boss. Whatever you say."

Finishing his smoke, Gnasher looked around for Aldo.

Aldo was nowhere in sight.

"How long does it take to get a bloody torch? It's no use hiding; show your ugly face and take the bollocking like a man." Gnasher raised his voice.

No response.

The Moon broke free from the clouds, revealing a cluster of dark figures, scurrying behind the car.

Aldo hadn't heard the Boss's threats. More significantly, he'd never know if Gnasher would have carried out Big Errol's orders, or as everyone in the syndicate thought, shit out of it at the last minute. Matter of fact, Aldo's *knowing* days had ended; '*The Pack*' had claimed him for supper.

Gnasher approached the driver's door.

"WHAT THE---" The rest of his words stayed in his mouth; the sight before him made him speechless.

Grunting like pigs in swill, a h uddle of feminine shaped beasts frenziedly fed on A ldo's body, blood spurting out of gaping incisions in the man's body.

"Hey...Put him down you...you...weirdo's." Bang...Bang, Gnasher fired over the heads of the quartet.

Hideous squeals filled the air.

One more 'Bang' and the hand that held the gun lay at its

owner's feet, severed by the machete wielded by the fur-coated fat blonde.

"You effin-" Were the last words spoken by Howard James Langham – affectionately known as Gnasher to his friends. He'd never know if, push came to shove, he would have done as he was told, and shot Karl, his best mate. Gnasher had suffered the same fate as Aldo and had joined the big boys in Gangster Heaven, or Hell…whichever.

Audrey claimed Gnasher as her first trophy. No more than fourteen years old, the youngest member of 'The Pack' had decapitated her victim. She'd wear goggles next time; the explosion of blood from his neck had momentarily blinded her. She needed an extra *wack*, to fully sever the head. Poor show, she'd get some abuse later.

*****

I struggled in the denseness of the wood; thick undergrowth impeded my escape. And the *noise*. Every twig I trod on shouted, *he's here*.

I stumbled into a body-sized crater. Getting up, I heard gunfire, coming from the direction of the car.

What was that all about?

Crawling to within a dozen yards of the car, I lifted my head to see what was happening.

A group of people milled around two dark shapes lying on the ground near the boot.

A woman with short black hair held a torch in one hand and a lump of…something, in the other.

Pools of what looked like blood where everywhere.

Two big women I recognised from outside the pub were fighting over the possession of what looked like a human leg. A smaller…*person*, had a ball shaped object in her hand. She carried it like a handbag. A dark liquid dripped from its base.

No. No. My inner voice screamed. That's Gnasher's head.

I catapulted my last meal onto the grass.

Several deep breaths later, I frantically looked for an escape route. It would be difficult, but if I could avoid detection in the forest, The Dog and Hare could only be a short walk away. Even allowing for the dense, dark terrain, I should be able to make it there in ten minutes or so, providing...

The howls grew louder. They didn't sound human. I was familiar with the wailing sounds of human suffering. As second in command, I'd sent many a poor sod to the hospital, and other places I didn't want to think about in my present circumstances...all courtesy of the Sheffield Godfather, Errol Smythe.

Claudia, the boss's young wife, called him Big Errol; for reasons known only to herself of course. The name stuck.

The man was a bastard. *Yes* and *no*, black and white, were his only guidelines.

"I'll give it back. I only borrowed the money to pay for the abortion." I remembered our last conversation as I approached the lights of the pub.

According to my watch, it was five past midnight; would the landlord have locked up and gone to bed?

My heart skipped a beat.

The main entrance was in darkness; the door locked.

The only light came from the door round the side.

"That was effin close," I said, pushing the door open.

My elation died immediately; the room was a dump. A string of low wattage bulbs tried their best to camouflage just how dilapidated the place had become.

A round, copper covered table, surrounded by five chairs that had seen better days, stood in the debris of furniture and broken glass. The smell of stale beer attacked my eyes and nostrils.

In the far corner, was a bar; an old, grey haired man stood at the bar, polishing a half pint glass with a cloth I wouldn't have wiped my shoes with.

Rushing towards him, I shouted, "Lock all the doors and phone the police; there's some mad women out there killing people."

Eyes bulging out of his sunken face, he sneered; black and broken teeth slavered as he spoke. "Oh dear…have the girls been naughty? I must have a w ord with them. Please make yourself comfortable; they shouldn't be long. Can I offer you a last drink?"

Power Cut

"Severe weather warning. A low-pressure front is approaching the Peak District. Six inches of snow are expected to fall on Kinder Scout in the next twelve hours. Residents in the area from Hathersage to Edale are particularly at risk as local temperatures could plummet to minus 20 degrees–"

"Turn that doom and gloom off…it's depressing." Fiona scowled at the TV. "Thank goodness we did our big shop on Friday; we won't have to eat the cat for at least a month."

Jim laughed and did as he was told…what else? "Can we eat the good stuff first?"

"That depends on whether you're a good boy or not."

"Aren't I always?" He made a grab for her.

"Stop it will–" Was as far as she got before he pressed his lips onto her warm, open mouth.

Fiona writhed in his embrace.

The kiss ended.

Sliding her wet lips up her partner's neck, she hungrily nibbled his right earlobe.

Jim loved the nibbling, responding with low and primitive moans.

"Enough of that; save it until later. Go and set the table please…*and* use a clean tablecloth." She pushed him away.

"You sound just like my mother. Where have you hidden the linen this week?"

"The same place as always…in the dresser."

Shaking his head, he clumsily ferreted through the neatly folded linen.

Meow. Freddy, the latest adopted stray, brushed Jim's leg.

"Honey Bun, feed the cat, I'm busy."

"And I'm not?" Fiona turned off the oven. "Men!"

Job done, he sat at the table, knife and fork at the ready.

"Idle sod. Get off your arse and do something."

"Yes Master. Speak and it shall be done."

"Open the wine. That white one we got from Morrison's last week. It will go nicely with the fish pie."

"What's for afters?"

"Home-made Dutch-apple-pie. My mother's own special recipe." She blew him a kiss.

"Did the lights just flicker?" Jim looked at the ceiling light.

"Sure did my love. Better get the candles out."

The lights went out.

"Bugger. It might have waited 'till I was ready." Using the cigarette lighter in his pocket, he managed to find the bunch of candles. He lit two of them and placed them on t op of the television. "That's not too bad, and we have got the open fire."

They sat, eating and talking as if dining in their favourite restaurant. The subdued lighting – courtesy of the power-cut – actually added a romantic atmosphere to the occasion.

"This reminds me of our first posh meal together." He held her hands across the table. "Do you remember the occasion?"

"Sure do, Casanova. Lennie's fish bar. The sit down section. You certainly knew how to treat a girl in those days."

They laughed.

"A toast to you, my princess. May we always be as happy as we are now."

"The dishes will have to wait until…whenever." She gave a shrug. "The electric could be off all night; what do you suggest we do for entertainment?"

"Well…"

"Darling, I do love you, but we can't be shagging all night long." She placed her hands on her hips…the intended *serious* look quickly dissolved into a wicked smile.

"I know…I Spy. That's a good game." Jim produced an exaggerated wink worthy of first prize in any 'Gurning' competition.

"Before we start." She pouted. "I'm not taking my clothes off; it's too cold without the central heating."

Hand in hand, they moved across to the rug in front of the open fire.

"Sit here, it's more comfortable." He patted his thighs.

"I'm alright here, thank you very much. Okay, come on then, you can start, and please try to be serious. I'm not playing if you act silly."

The glow from the fire cast eerie shadows around the room.

"I Spy with my little eye, something beginning with...cee."

"Cooker."

"Cheat. You saw me looking at it."

"All's fair in love and I Spy." She giggled; she liked to win.

"Your turn. And *I* won't look." He stuck his tongue out.

"I Spy with my little eye…*Freddy*."

"Fiona, you're supposed to give me the first letter, not the entire…oh shit."

Then he saw what she was looking at. "What's up with that bloody cat?"

Freddy sat on the table; frothy lumps dripping from his bared teeth. Wild, glaring eyes, glowing in the dimly lit room.

Jim jumped up a nd ran into the dark kitchen. "Shit, I've stubbed me toe," he squealed.

The power came back on just as he found the bread knife.

Lights rekindled, he turned to face the four-legged beast.

Meow.

"Aah; bless him. Look, he's covered in the whipped cream I'd made for the apple pie." Fiona wiped the cat's face with a tissue.

Jim brandished the long, serrated knife in the air. "Well, the 'devil cat's' just had a lucky escape; that's one of its nine lives gone out the window. He's also got the pudding; what do I get?"

"The icing on the cake…big boy. It's upstairs. Come on. I'll show you."

Storyteller

"Are you sitting comfortably? Then I'll begin."

"Oh no you don't," I said to the intruder who'd been hiding behind the old oak tree. "I heard all of them kiddy-winks stories when I was a nipper. And anyway, I was studying...so bugger off."

The old woman pursed her lips, crossed her arms and fired a salvo of TUTS right into my face. "Too big for Noddy and Rupert; why, shame on you Paddo."

"Please don't call me that." I put the Racing Post on the grass and turned to face the pain in my ears. She stood as bold as brass, the sun silhouetting her frame. Not a pretty sight; she looked like a gargoyle on fire. "Bloody hell, it's Thora Hird. What are you doing here? Have you escaped from a pantomime?" I had to smile.

"No I haven't, you cheeky monkey. You don't know what's good for you; sit down and forget about the horse racing for a bit. Tell you what Paddo–"

"I told you not to call me that...it brings back the memories."

"Memories are the building blocks of the soul." Thora sat by my side. "Good and bad...they're all important."

"Bollocks; who told you that load of old rubbish?"

"If your Mam could hear you now she'd wash your mouth out."

"If my Mam was here she'd tell you to piss off. She liked a bet on the gee-gees as much as I do. She loved to study the form-book did my Mam."

"Come on lad...help me out. I've been sent down here to convert you. They're not too keen on gamblers up there." With an exaggerated flutter of her batwing eyelashes, she pointed the rainbow striped stick upwards.

I looked up at the sky. "Are you completely mad? Birds don't give a flying pig about my gambling habits."

"Silly boy…I'm talking about God. He's worried about you."

"He wasn't worried about me last week at Aintree. That nag falling at the last fence did me out of thousands of pounds."

"Money doesn't interest the Celestial Realms." Thora did the rapid eyelash thing again.

"Have you nothing better to do? Get back to the theatre. The show must go on."

"How can I, ya daft ha'peth? I'm dead."

"I thought you looked under the weather the last time I saw you on the telly." I put my glasses on. "Yes…you have deteriorated quite a bit."

"Very funny. Well…Now that's sorted, can I interest you in a story? Anything at all…except one of them mucky ones…I don't do smut." Pursing her lips even harder, she wriggled her shoulders.

"OK. I've got a hour to kill until the first race at Ascot…get on with it."

"Get on with it–" She shook the multi-coloured stick within inches of my face. "If not for you, you ungrateful little beggar, I could be playing farm yard snap with Compo."

"But he's dead as well." I scratched my head. "Time out, Thora…I'm at your disposal…Honest, I'm being serious."

She withdrew the stick, adjusted her black, horn-rimmed glasses and repeated the shoulder and lips mannerisms. "Crime, Adventure or Sci-Fi. No messing about…you've blown the other options."

"You know, Thora, I always liked that book about that Beau Geste chap …but the end was crap. Can you tell me the story with a different ending?"

She rose into the air, hovering two feet above my head like a helicopter in drag.

"P.C. Wren would have my guts for garters if I altered the ending. No…Beau dies and that's it."

"Well…Can we compromise? Can he be very ill and end up needing mobility aids for a while?"

"Get back to your horse racing, you heathen. There's no hope for you." She shot like a missile into the clear blue sky.

Bye bye Thora.

What would she have thought if I'd asked for my second choice? Alien…with a new ending of course. Ripley would be sucked out of the spaceship instead of the monster.

Thanks Stanley

My own boots, at last. No more poxy school pumps...you never know who wore them last. It could have been stickky-ike ; 'our Michael,' to his widowed mum Edna. We of the third form had cruelly renamed him because of his profuse sweating and insatiable appetite for liquorice sticks.

Now I'll show them. Just watch me perform with the latest Stanley Mathews football boots. Real leather mind you. This pair were out of the 'junior professional' range. The dogs bollocks of the football world; far superior to the bog standard ones. Mine had extra studs fitted, giving more grip...and the latest super long laces. Dad told me, 'Nothing's too good for you John,' and paid an extra five bob to prove it.

I can understand now why some of the soppy girls in our class get all excited by perfumes and the smell of flowers. Each time I put the new boots on, the musky, sweet smell of leather brings a huge smile to my face. I'd better watch who sees me sniffing and grinning, it could put a bit of a dent in my macho image; you can't be too careful at eleven years old.

I can just hear Blakey shouting, 'you played a blinder John', as I come off the field amid a rapturous applause from the crowd as I make history: the first left back to score ten goals in a game.

I can dream can't I? Blakey, better known as Mr George Alwynn Blake, assistant headmaster and senior sports teacher of Hamlet Lane Secondary Modern, always said I was a u seless sod with two left feet and no chance of ever making the school team. Stanley and me will show him. We'll show everybody. Just you wait and see.

The Accident

This is the true – well most of it anyway – account of my wife's accident on Dec. 24th 2006...Christmas Eve.

We had called at our daughter's house to deliver presents, cards, etc. Coming downstairs from the toilet – steep and treacherous is a fair description – she fell from top to bottom, breaking her leg in the process.

The ambulance duly arrived and promptly transferred her to the A and E department at Calow Hospital.

Her extensive period of incapacity, the use of walking aids – the wheelchair in particular – and the slow, very slow recovery, are not mentioned. That would be another story, indeed, a book.

*****

"Send for the ambulance." Sandra yelled.

"What happened?" John placed the knife and fork on the table and clumsily swallowed the rather large piece of pork sausage being savoured at the time. Not just ordinary sausage either but the REAL McCoy, made with 90% meat. He couldn't eat that *cheapo crammo* variety on offer at two for the price of one at Tesco; they contained too many spices and herbs for his delicate palate.

"I think I've broken my leg." Diane looked at the distorted limb – pointing in the wrong direction – trying her best to come to terms with the excruciating pain erupting from the shattered bones.

She'd experienced the trauma of childbirth on four occasions. The youngest – a girl of course – was a forceps delivery...no epidural mind you. Even so, she wasn't prepared for the wave after wave of agonies as she lay, very unladylike, at the bottom of the stairs.

"I've ruined my Ann Harvey skirt; I've only worn it twice." Sixty the following June, Diane liked to think she was still 'with it'. She loved the knee length Paisley patterned creation she'd bought from Debenhams.

Sandra's husband, Maurice, had phoned the emergency services, who had assured him that the response time from Chesterfield was ten minutes…*maximum*.

"I only let go for a second." Diane sobbed, looking at Sandra in the vain hope that her youngest daughter could wave a magic wand, reverse time, and avert the stupid error made at the top of the stairs.

"We'll have to sell the house and buy one with a downstairs toilet; it's like descending the North face of the Eiger." Sandra blamed herself for the fall.

"Christmas Eve of all times," John said to his wife of forty years. "Who'll get the dinner ready?" At a loss as to what he could do to help or comfort his childhood sweetheart, he picked up the last piece of sausage.

They'd been through many difficult situations together, but nothing as traumatic as this. Well…that is unless you counted the time Diane had gone into the male toilets in Monastir airport. The angry mob almost lynched her. John could still hear the bloodcurdling voice of the Arabs. 'Infidel, infidel' they shouted as they chased Diane around the luggage carousel.

Now it would have been a very different matter if her car had broken down. You see, John was always, 'Messing about with mechanical things'; Diane's interpretation of his love for internal combustion engines and their efficiency. Unfortunately she had no respect or acceptance of his HNC in Mechanical Engineering.

Andy, the senior of the two paramedics, instantly diagnosed

a compound fracture of the right tibia. "Give the lady some morphine," he said to his mate Phil before saying, "you'll be all right now darling, just keep calm," to the anxious patient.

"You try to keep calm with a smashed up leg that feels like an atom bomb is going off inside the bloody thing." Diane squealed. She stared at Andy, observing that the small framed man – no more than nine stone wet through – had the biggest bogey in the world trying to escape from his hairy left nostril.

If that falls on me *he'll* have a broken leg, Diane mentally promised, inwardly shuddering at the thought of such a gross object coming into contact with her Olay pampered flesh. And if it fell on her Monsoon blouse, she would have no option but to kill him – it's so difficult getting a size twenty in anything modern; she'd trawled the country for this one.

"Mama, why are you crying?" Abigail, the youngest grand-child, said as she stroked Diane's head.

The morphine kicked in. Diane looked at Abigail through the pink mist of euphoria and said, "Santa's coming tonight. You'd better be a good girl...and no fighting with Jack," before slumping back onto Andy's chest. The last thing she saw before her eyes surrendered to the drugs, was the angelic face of Abigail with a stream of tears rolling down her cheek, and the foreign body escaping from the paramedic's nose hanging within a few millimetres of her grandchild's, long, golden hair.

The Dream

I'm falling. I'm f-a-l-l-i-n-g.

The wind hammered my face as the ground rushed to meet me.

The blur transfigured into a tapestry of blue and green.

Large, mushroom shapes transformed into leafy canopies – natures umbrella for the forest I was about to smash into.

I prepared myself for the worst...in a matter of seconds I would crash into the landscape.

But I didn't. Instead...I found myself hovering over a herd of deer. Occupying a huge expanse of grass, they casually grazed, oblivious to my presence.

Summer fragrances filled my Soul. Bees and butterflies attended the flowers.

Wondrous sounds caressed my ears. Symphonies of bird songs, the rustling of gentle breezes in the tree-tops and the tinkling sounds of water blended as one voice. Nature's chorus...sweet and clear.

I floated...drifted from flora to fauna.

My senses exploded into a magical, super-awareness.

A never-ending range of mountains filled my panorama. Snow covered and rugged, they forced themselves into the clouds...vanishing like wraiths into oblivion.

Higher and higher, like an eagle riding a thermal, I soared. Powerful, majestic...the king of the sky.

Atop of the world, I surveyed my dominion. Spread before me was Armageddon. Flames consumed the earth. Cries of the suffering and the dying demanded my attention. The sun hid itself behind a dense black cloud. Darkness consumed the World.

I woke up. Tears ran like acid down my face.

The Holiday

It should have been a relaxed holiday. Seven glorious days of doing nothing more strenuous than taking the top off the factor twenty sun screen. It should have been...but it wasn't.

You see...The brochure lied. 'Within view of the sea, and a short walking distance' were not true. Yes, the pretty cove with gentle waves breaking on the shore *was* visible, but it was more than a mile away from the apartment.

What 'Zorba's guide to the Med' didn't say, was that you had to sit on the hotel roof to have any chance of looking over the forest of pine trees surrounding the complex, and full protective gear was required to traverse the stretch of land known locally as 'The Wilderness.'

Giant thistles covered the terrain...swaying gently in the breeze, like drunken Triffids guarding the broken glass and discarded furniture from the newly renovated Ocean View Palace.

Dominic loved the daily circumnavigation of 'The Wilderness.' He'd done flora and fauna of the Tropics in his final year at Swadlincote Grammar School and was fascinated by the many species of snakes and lizards hiding in the mountain of refuse. By the end of the week, he'd identified ten reptiles...four of them venomous.

If he set out after breakfast, taking the packed lunch alternative to the all-inclusive option, he could reach the desired beach in just under the hour...provided he didn't slip and fall into the snake pit.

After his first attempt, abandoned due to nausea, he decided to take an extra bath towel from his room. This was adjudged to be essential equipment with a dual role: protection from the swarms of mosquitoes and a filtration unit to mask the putrid smells emanating from the dead cats rotting in the stagnant paddling pool.

The sandy beach was deserted. Soft and ultra-fine, it ran through his fingers like talcum powder.

The turquoise sea was calm, clear and inviting.

The jellyfish were plentiful, huge and threatening.

Laptops, Lockets and Cards

"Thank you, Richard, it's just what I wanted; a perfect early birthday present." Clarissa smiled, her pale brown eyes radiating her happiness. "The old laptop has seen better days; it's becoming a right pain in the posterior."

"You're very welcome, Morgana. Anything to keep you happy."

"Don't be cheeky or I'll have to put a spell on you." She gave him a look usually saved for the paying customers.

Richard crossed his arms to form a crucifix. "Back off, woman, or I'll spray you with holy water."

He laughed…she didn't.

"It looks like that sad looking object in the corner could do with some water, holy or not." Clarissa nodded in the direction of the withered remains of a poinsettia. "You're neglecting the poor thing…I know how it feels."

"*Poor thing*? You little hypocrite." Richard stood up, catching the desk with his knee. "You looked like you'd swallowed a deadly poison when you opened Mum's present. I remember you saying, 'she knows I don't like potted plants.' That was the last Christmas we had with my Mother."

"Confession time, Richard. Yes, I was disappointed, and for a very good reason. I thought that your wonderful mother–"

"Be careful what you say, she might be listening." He looked at the ceiling.

"Don't mock me, Richard…Anyway, back to what I was just saying. I wrongly assumed that your mum was getting me a silver locket and chain from the Argos catalogue. She'd asked me if I preferred the Belcher Link chain or the Figaro. Even asked if I spelled my name with one S or two."

Richard moved towards Clarissa. "What do y ou think of this?" He placed his sketch in front of her.

"Fabulous; your eye for detail is awesome, but–"

"But what?"

"I love your ideas for the business cards. The tarot images are impressive and the astral signs theme works really well, but…To be honest, I need to get the template into the laptop and make a few adjustments. I can't scan it in, the resolution of the Epson flatbed you bought me two years ago isn't high enough for the job. Look, I really don't want to upset you, but you're living in the past. The modern way to create business cards is in Microsoft Publisher. Manipulation is easy; font size and style can be changed in seconds. The choices are endless."

"Hmm." He turned away. "You know I don't do computers."

"You're just like that vintage, pianoforte in the lounge. Old fashioned and–"

He spun back to face his wife. "Go on, s ay it. *Obsolete.* That's what you think; you might as well say it."

"Richard…Behave…And *do not* put words in my mouth. I was going to say old fashioned and a little out of tune. Technology is the way forward. Computers are wonderful. Indeed…a godsend. They save time and make life so much easier. This new laptop will be a lot quicker than the old one. Oh dear." She rubbed her chin. "According to the information on the box, this model has got Windows Seven installed. All of my friends on Face- book say it's useless…as bad as Vista. You know how much I struggled with the internet when I had Vista installed over XP in my old laptop. I'll have to fetch Gerald in to change the operating system yet again. Bother…it's such a nuisance."

"Well then, in that case you may as well keep the old one. I'll take the new one back to PC World and get you that silver locket and chain you wanted from Argos. It is Clarissa with one

R and and two S's isn't it. Right? Would you like any more words inscribed?"

Clarissa's eyes narrowed. "Yes please darling." She hissed through closed teeth. "Have them put, **Wife of Richard, who died suddenly**. Put tomorrow's date; *then rush home*."

"That is not funny, Clarissa."

"No, and you're not either. Most of OUR money comes from the private readings I do on my website. You scoff at my work, but you like the extra money it brings in. I can't manage without a reliable computer. It's like having a personal friend at my beck and call."

"Is that why you sometimes call it a bastard?"

"Enough…Richard. Enough. Let's move forward. Together if possible. When I've installed all of my software and files into the new machine, I'll show you how to use the latest business card creator. With your artistic skills and my techno abilities, I'm confident we can produce a professional and successful product."

"And what does the Spirit World think of your plans for 'Morgana's World of Light'?" He couldn't fully suppress a chuckle.

Eyes narrowed into slits. Clarissa gave him a withering scowl.

Plucking her favourite pack of Tarot cards from her handbag – the ones with angels on the back – she said, "Sit down, Richard. I'll ask them."

Shuffled and dealt, the seventy-eight cards lay face down on the coffee table she used for her private sittings.

"Well. What do the higher realms have to say?" He masked his smile with his hand.

She looked at the five-card spread; it was never wrong. "I've got the Magician and Fool sat together, with the Two of Cups and Three of Wands reversed."

"Is that good?"

"It was…until the Knight of Swords appeared."

"What does that mean?"

"It's a warning. Trouble is coming. Turbulence, pain and destruction surround our future."

"When?"

"Soon, Richard. Very soon…if you don't stop mucking about and make me a coffee. I'll have the Gold Blend please; I've gone off the Espresso."

The Obesity Debate

"The clinic is running a little late, Mr Burgess. Dr Johnson was called to an emergency in Resus. Dr Ossigambo is standing in. He's scrubbing up...shouldn't be too long."

Phil – Mr Burgess to the vision of beauty called Staff Nurse Julia Wallis – was not pleased with the delay.

"Is that the chap who looks like Frank Bruno?" Phil queried, looking over his horn-rimmed spectacles.

"He has letters after his name," Julia responded.

"I hope they're not R.I.P. I'm only here for a consultation." Grinning, he took a longer look at Julia Wallis. Oh yes – he thought – I'd like to see her scrub up.

Queen's Mill Orthopaedic Department wasn't renowned for its reading material. The enforced delay on top of a full clinic, limiting the choice drastically. The selection now placed before Phil to relieve the boredom was either the NHS information pamphlets, Yachting Monthly or Mother and Baby.

'Am I in the right clinic?' He pondered.

Bored out of his mind, he reluctantly considered the ultimate and last resort...*THE PAMPHLETS*.

Today's offerings were not very tempting. One of them gave a step by step guide as to the treatment and aftercare of gangrene; another one covered the progressive stages of syphilis...all in glorious technicolor.

Julia called the man sitting opposite to Phil.

SAVED. 'God bless him, he's left his newspaper'. Phil was pleased. Now, The Morning Herald wasn't exactly his favourite daily drivel from Fleet Street, but hey ho, beggars can't be choosers.

The sins and corruption's of the world exploded from the front page. David Beckham was accused for the umpteenth time this year of infidelity, and yet another member of Parliament was forced to admit that he was gay.

Politicians admit nothing. The man was caught with his pants down…literally. Phil never quite understood why they called such people gay; homosexuals, that's what they are. Gay was how Gordon MacRae and Doris Day had felt 'On Moonlight Bay'. And as for Beckham, there's no wonder the poor chap is always on the injured bench. According to the papers, he scores more off the field than on. I'm not reading any more of that rubbish…Phil turned the page. The headline: 'Foot and mouth is spreading' caught his attention. Making a mental note to get some tinned sausages in just in case, he turned to the horoscope page. Not that he believed any of the Astral rubbish, but being a Taurus he thought it wouldn't hurt to have a look. Before he could read 'the daily stars', his eyes locked onto a small heading on the opposite page.

The Obesity Debate. A 20th Century Epidemic.

We used to call them fat or chubby…the Americans label them obese. We copy them Yanks in everything. I blame Tony Blair, he was far too chummy with Bush. *An Epidemic*? That's what measles and influenza are. How do you catch obesity? By rubbing bellies with someone? I'd like to rub bellies with Staff Nurse Wallis. Phil Burgess's imagination was in full flow.

There had always been something sensual about Phil's image of the Nursing Profession…the female variety of course, a rear gunner he wasn't. He blamed this fixation on the Carry On films; Babs Windsor did a lot of the damage.

He studied the black and white graph with your height on one axis, your weight on the other. According to the experts, if the resultant figure, your Body Mass Index, BMI to snobs who like abbreviations, was over thirty, you were officially obese, and needed to join your local Weight Watchers Club as soon as they opened. Nowhere did it mention exceptions, such as big bones. Momma Burgess always said Phil was big-boned. What if you where constipated? You know, not been to the toilet for a week or more; or, in a woman's case, the wrong time of the month. Did that also apply to homosexuals? For sure, Phil's imagination was in full swing.

"Mrs Hardy."

Phil watched the old woman at the end of his row follow the nurse and calculated that he must be next.

Phil decided that the only good thing about the room was the digital clock. Wrinkled, glossy pictures, scattered randomly across the walls, were no better than *THE PAMPHLETS*, equally warranting an X certificate. Multi-coloured plates showed actual surgical procedures, sickeningly portraying the effects of diseased organs removed for disposal or for scientific research by the pathology guys. Phil shuddered at the thought...he'd seen less blood and disembowelments in The Hammer House of Horrors films he watched at the cinema.

Capping it all off, a prosthetic arm hung from a cobwebbed light fitting. Pointing in the direction of the toilets, a large signet ring with a silver letter Z, sat on one of the fingers.

'Changing Rooms' should be invited to work their magic here. Laurence Llewelyn-Bowen would have a field day.' Phil's dream machine motored on.

"Are you alright?" Phil smiled at the young Janet Street Porter clone sitting opposite.

"I wouldn't be here if I was," she exploded, attempting to wave her bandaged arm.

End of that conversation.

Sooner than risk another fruitless discussion with the Ben Stiller look-alike sat next to him, Phil returned to the paper and Mystic Mary's forecast.

"Not a good day for Virgo's," he said to the Janet woman.

She gave him a filthy look.

'Aries…highly sexed and experimental. Faithful while in love, but if love begins to fade, they start to look around.' He savoured this intimate information direct from the heavenly realms. Staff Nurse Wallis...she looks like she could be an Aries.

"Mr Philip Burgess…Room Two."

How could she be so informal when he knew her innermost secrets?

"And can you leave a urine sample before you go."

"I think I already have…all over my chips," he chuntered.

The Frank Bruno look-alike doctor was a p leasant sort of chap, such a pity he didn't speak much English. Student Nurse Mary O'Neil controlled the verbal interchange. Interpreter for the day, she was fluent in Irish and Brunoese; somewhere in the middle, they managed to find a common understanding.

The relief consultant studied the X-rays and notes from Mr Phil Burgess's previous appointment with Dr Johnson. Speaking in a refined, soft voice, he uttered a mouthful of strange words.

Student Nurse O'Neil translated..."Jesus but ya have a terrible knee there."

Phil didn't think O'Neil had a future as an interpreter, but admired her enthusiasm. "Can you suggest anything other than painkillers? I'm taking so many tablets that I rattle when I walk." He asked in a voice a bit too loud.

Obviously eager to find the cause of the phenomena, Bruno's eyes' lit up as he swung his stethoscope into action. He dictated his conclusions to the interpreter.

A worried looking Nurse O'Neil said, "Yo can have de knee capped, but Holy Mary yo's very young for a procedure like that."

"I'm getting out of here whilst I still have two legs." Phil hastily pulled his pants up.

"Have you been discharged, Mr Burgess?" Staff Nurse Wallis asked as he passed by.

"That's the best impression I've ever seen of Long John Silver," Ben Stiller shouted as Phil attempted to run down the corridor.

To this day, Phil Burgess does not know how he ended up in Ward Four, the Busted Limbs Annexe. He remembers the wet floor notice, but nothing else. Apparently – according to Janet Street Porter and Ben Stiller – he glided gracefully down the corridor on one leg, like a professional ice skater, scattering all before him like skittles. Gravity unkindly brought him down to earth with a thump; painfully depositing him amongst the wheelchairs outside of Ward Ten.

Josie, Phil's wife, visited him that evening.

He was as comfortable as could be expected. Matron said the knee-cap replacement had gone well and that Dr Johnson was pleased with everything. Phil could be discharged in five days…barring any complications, of course. However, an appointment must be made at reception for him to see the dietician as the pre op tests had revealed a BMI of thirty-one. Much too high, a health hazard and a serious handicap to his mobility with the walking aids he now relied upon.

The Package

"Please put the package on the belt, Sir."

This is where it gets interesting. Do I look guilty? Of course I don't, if I did, this man mountain of a security guard would hang me by my feet until I confessed. Right…I'll bluff it out…look nonchalant.

"Thank you Sir, go to the end of the conveyor please."

Phew, that's the first hurdle cleared. Keep calm and don't sweat whatever you do. I made a bee line for the nearest bar. "Large Bud, please," I said. "And a pack of Marlboros." Yes…that should help the nerves.

Where do all these giants come from? Man mountain security guard's clone passed me my order.

"That'll be ten dollars if you please, Sir."

These Yanks sure have manners.

Good…Flight AA446 to Miami was on time; just over an hour to take off. What next? Should I go to Departures now or wait for the announcement from the Tannoy?

'Get it over with…why postpone the inevitable? You're sure to be caught.' My inner voice screamed at me. I took a deep drag from the cigarette. Yes, I know smoking is bad for the health, but at this moment in time I have far worse things to consider; any possible future problems involving the dreaded C word looked to be an excellent alternative to my present predicament.

I sneaked a look at the baggage monitor screen. Even the scanned image looked suspicious.

'It's over. They'll pull you to one side and cuff you like a common criminal and make a right commotion. Then the guard will get personal with your flesh.' My inner self was giving me a right tongue-lashing.

God, they can't. They can't. I mustn't be arrested.

"Thank you Sir. Have a great vacation." Mrs Man Mountain flashed her pearly whites.

Nearly over. Someone up there is definitely looking after me. To be more precise...looking after Glenda.

That's it. I'll board late. If any of the flight crew ask about the package I'll say I want to keep it by my seat...that the overhead lockers are full. Yes...that sounds plausible.

Am I being watched? Don't get paranoid, Bob, not now it's almost over.

"This is the last call for Flight AA446 to Miami International. All passengers remaining please make your way immediately to Gate 7."

Okay...I'll mingle with that family at the end of the line. Perfect, the young boy is acting up. Nobody will pay me any attention.

Great. It worked.

Keep cool. Only 50 metres of tarmac and it's finally over.

In the blink of an eye, the whole scene erupted. A platoon of America's finest appeared from behind the nearest Airbus 320.

Two dog handlers struggled to control their snarling black beasts straining at their tethers.

Frozen to the spot, I fought to keep control of my bladder.

"Place it on the ground, then step to one side. Hands in the air. NOW." Man Mountain with a serious attitude screamed, holding an automatic rifle inches away from my head.

The heavily armoured officer brushed me to one side. Picking up the package, he looked to his superiors. "All secure, Captain. All safe and secure."

"Well now, Robert...do you mind if I call you Bob? What have you been up to? Don't you like the U.S. of A?" The officer smirked.

"I had no choice. They made me do it," I stammered.

"Glenda Montoya sure is a sweet gal aint she?"

"What? You know Glenda?" I gazed in amazement at the grinning Captain.

"Sure do…she's on our list; surveillance know her well. The Red Parrot on Nixon Drive is her hunting ground. A real looker is Glenda."

"She said she loved me. I took her everywhere; bought her a ring. She stayed with me all week. That bunch of thugs said they'd kill her if I didn't do as they said." I shook my head. What was going on?

"We ought to thank you, Bob. We snared Yusef Benagi this time. He was watching you from the gangway; holding everybody back with his stopping and starting. We assumed you were meant to pass him the guns when the plane was at altitude."

"Why did you let me get this far?" I couldn't stop shaking my head.

"We had to be sure he was getting on t he plane. He disappeared from his usual haunts weeks ago. We wondered what he was up to; you flushed him out for us. You were spotted with Glenda. We guessed something was up but his disguise and false passport fooled us all. The Senior Air Stewardess reported his suspicious activity. Up and down he was, like a Yo-Yo. He obviously thought you'd bottled it. You did leave it very late to board."

The Scoop6

"I'm having the Full English Breakfast…what about you two?" Brett Simms placed The Sporting Life on the table and waited for an answer.

"Yes please, and bring me two sachets of brown sauce." Howard Vardy replied. "What are you having Jan?"

"Sausage cob please. Oh, and a portion of mushrooms?"

Wetherspoons was busy. The recent enforcement of the No Smoking order meant that the entire gamut of delicious culinary smells were now undiluted by the foul stench of nicotine. Appetite inducing aromas filled the room; mercilessly attacking newly awakened taste buds.

The ultimate fast food weapon and Nemesis of Weight Watchers, BACON, was fighting its corner. It really didn't matter whether you liked bacon or not, just the smell of it made you hungry.

"Six to four Quasimodo is pinching money; it's sure to start at odds on." Brett gulped a mouthful of strong tea. "Timeform have him ten points clear. It's my banker bet today. What do you think Jan?"

"It certainly looks good, but he does make the odd mistake, and Kempton's a graveyard for bad jumpers. I'm leaving that race alone. I really like Candid Peel's chances at Lingfield. She hated the going last week at Warwick, *and* she's a course and distance winner; excellent each way value."

"I bloody hate Lingfield; it's like a dog track. Them all-weather courses are crap. Bookies benefits, that's what they are." Howard said to his wife.

Janet and Howard Vardy rarely agreed on racing matters. Jan liked her flat racing…Howard preferred the National Hunt. He studied the form like his life depended on it whilst she used a mixture of common sense and intuition.

"You might as well stick a pin in the paper," he used to say to her. Used to. Not anymore. He had to swallow his pride on several occasions. The most humbling time being when Jan backed a 20/1 no-hoper to beat Howard's short priced favourite in a selling race at Southwell. 'It only won because mine got boxed in. The jockey should have been sacked; even I could have won on that horse,' he'd argued.

'I told you not to back it. Never lay the odds, especially in sellers; unwritten first rule of gambling.' A self-satisfied smile enshrouded her face as she stuffed the winnings into her purse.

Breakfast finished, Jan looked in her handbag for a mirror. Life's a cruel bitch, she thought, carefully replenishing the lipstick on her diminishing pout. Botox before much longer, she sighed.

Placing his glasses on the table, Brett said, "There's a record Scoop6 carry-over today, over a million pounds. It might end up making a couple of million more; we could all use some of that. I wouldn't normally consider it, but I have to admit that this one is very tempting; two of the races are almost walkovers. Shall we have a go?"

"We've heard all that before, haven't we Howard?" Jan gave her husband a wink and a knowing nod.

"You'll never let me forget that race, will ya? I still say you were lucky."

"Stop it, you two. I'm having a go anyhow, but if we stood in we could combine a few more horses and share the winnings. We'd stand a much better chance." Brett opened the paper to the Kempton page. "You've got to speculate to accumulate."

Half an hour and extra drinks later, the trio had reached an agreement.

"Tommy Blue in the first and Quasimodo in the fifth are our bankers. Ok? Then we'll pick one horse each for the other four races." Jan looked from Brett to Howard.

"Agreed," said Howard.

"Agreed." Brett responded with a hint of reluctance.

"That combination will be £162 in total; £54 each. That's a lot of money." Jan repeated the facial sweep.

Howard took a sharp intake of breath. "Nothing ventured nothing gained. If we don't win anything, we'll have to go and stop at your Mother's for a week." He wiggled his eyebrows at his wife.

She didn't acknowledge the gesture.

They left Wetherspoons and walked across the road to Ladbrokes – a journey they'd shared for the last year.

The Vardy's were shy and didn't make friends easily, but surprisingly hit it off straight away with the flamboyant Brett Simms. A common interest in gambling, horse racing in particular, instantly united the trio. Any differences in class, education, temperament or even gender being immediately forgotten. Discussing the outcome of a race with a fellow loser, or better still, winner, bonded them together. Within a month, they where bosom buddies, sharing tips received from fellow punters and sometimes even secret information leaked directly from the stables…*supposedly.*

Brett was a compulsive gambler; lived for it. He would have a bet on two flies climbing up a wall, or on the next bus being yellow, blue or red.

A part time job in the mornings – something to do w ith driving – left the afternoons free for the booking office. Set in his ways, he followed a strict routine: Wetherspoons by noon, full English Breakfast with large tea and extra toast. He sat as close to the entrance as possible, devouring the Sporting Life as hungrily as his food. Ladbrokes by 1pm gave him time to chat with the regulars and exchange tips and information before placing his, 'Early Price' bets. He called these his 'Fun Bets';

four or five selections with odds of at least 10/1, in each way doubles. He never expected them all to win, but for a modest outlay of £20, he had the pleasure of watching them all compete. More often than not, he cleared his stake, sometimes winning a few hundred.

Saturday was for serious gambling. Brett liked to have one, sometimes two, win bets – maximum wager of £200. He religiously watched The Morning Line on Channel Four. The betting market movers often highlighted the so called 'triers'. Many a winner came from the interviews with guest trainers and jockeys. His Fun Bets today would be The Tote Scoop6. Sure, it was a bit of a lottery, and £54 was more than he usually laid out for his 'Fun Bets', but today's pay-out could be life-changing. By joining forces with Howard and Jan, multiple selections could be afforded, greatly increasing the possibility of a win.

Today's Scoop6 was from Kempton, Lingfield and Doncaster. The general consensus of the newspaper tipsters being that two of the races looked pretty much cut and dried and the Doncaster Sprint with nine runners had only three real challengers. However, the remaining three handicaps had lots of runners, and were wide open.

"You can't be serious, Jan? Rubber Duck and Troilus are bad enough, but Candid Peel…she was so far behind last week they had to send a search party out." Brett was not amused.

"My £54 buys me the right to choose any horses I want. I'm deferring to your…*better judgement*… on the two certainties." The look Jan gave her partners would have melted steel.

"She's right; leave her alone." Howard gave his selections to Brett.

"Sorry, Jan. Your money, your selections. I didn't mean to offend you." Brett completed the Scoop6 betting slip.

Tommy Blue hacked in; the short priced favourite led from

start to finish.

"That didn't take many out of the pool," Howard said to anyone in the stands who was listening.

The second race went to Brett's selection at 6/1. Then Howard came good with a storming 12/1 shot in the first handicap.

"That's better; I told you it liked this track." Howard jumped up and down. "There can only be a couple of thousand tickets left now."

Jan decided it was time for a lippy top up. Excusing herself, she went to the ladies' room.

"If this one goes in, we're laughing," Brett unconsciously pulled at his right earlobe.

"Come on my son, come on. That's the way to do it." Brett squealed as his selection won the Doncaster Sprint.

"That's four in the bag. What are you going to buy with your share, Jan? A new face?" Howard regretted the frivolity immediately.

"You stand need to talk, *Baldy*...you need a complete new head." Jan's broadside ended the conversation.

Then disaster struck. Quasimodo took one chance too many. Ten lengths clear coming to the final fence, he overjumped and slipped on landing. Tony McCoy's acrobatics kept him in the saddle but they lost so much ground that the outsider of the seven runners sailed by to beat him by a length.

"Don't say it, don't say it. I know...Bloody Kempton. He only had to clear the last. That was my banker. I blew £200 on that animal." Brett was not pleased. Neither were his partners, nor the eighteen hundred and fifty Scoop6 ticket holders mown down by the odds on favourite's mistake.

"That's the win pool well and truly destroyed," said Howard. "Only chance we have now is with the place pool."

The final leg was always going to be the most difficult race of the day. A twenty-three runner selling handicap at Lingfield, the punters nightmare.

True to form, it turned out to be the bookies benefit it looked on paper. The first four past the post all big priced outsiders. The winner started at 40/1.

The win pool of two and a half million pounds was not won, to be carried over to the next Saturday.

"Well…I hope that will teach the pair of you a lesson. There's no such thing as a certainty. Never lay odds on to your money…Dad always said it. But you can dry your tears now, boys; I've saved the day."

Smiling like a hyena with lockjaw, Jan looked in the mirror…instantly deciding that her share of the £745 placepot dividend would be spent wisely on the Botox treatment.

"Bless her, Candid Peel ran a s tormer, didn't she? You know…with a bit of luck in running, she might even have won. Never mind…third place was good enough for us…and there's always next week…I can't wait." Jan winked at her partners.

To Err is Human

"Where were you last night?" Trevor looked into his wife's, dull, bloodshot eyes.

"And what's it to you, 'Grumpy'? Don't pretend that you still care." Annabelle pushed a cigarette into her twisted mouth.

"That's it, bang another nail in your coffin?" Trevor switched on the extractor fan. "It bloody stinks in here. It's a pity you can't think of somebody else for a change. Jemma looks up to you…poor kid. What kind of example are you setting? Every Saturday morning it's the same old story; Mummy's transformed into a pathetic looking alky. You bloody tramp, have you no pride left?"

A scowl grew on Annabelle's ashen face. "Bastard," she slurred, almost ejecting the cigarette from her lips.

Then came the tears.

The scars on Annabelle's body *may* have faded, but the *incident* still festered in her husband's mind.

God help him, but Trevor still loved her; not many husbands would have stood by their wives in such scandalous circumstances.

"I'm going to Whitby; you have my mobile number if you really need me." He picked up the car keys from the worktop.

"Bring me some kippers. If I'm lucky I'll choke on the bones." She coughed.

He watched her slide her fingers through her thick, black hair.

Bella had beautiful hair. *Had*, using the past tense. Once long and well groomed, it now had the appearance of tangled seaweed.

Bella…when had he last called her Bella? Trevor couldn't

recall the occasion, it must have been before…

The scraping of his wife's chair on the tiled floor dragged him back to reality.

"Trevor," she said, "it's not like you think it is...you know, me going out on a Friday night. I'm not on the pull. Its just a girlie night out at the Red Squirrel. Tracy and Donna like to go there; we just have a bit of fun and a dance."

He so wanted to believe her; to trust her again. "Does *he* go there? Is he the, '*bit of fun*'?" Trevor couldn't even say the man's name.

"If you mean Nigel, then no, he doesn't. I heard that he moved away after the accident." She lowered her eyes. "I know what I did was wrong." She couldn't look at her husband. "I'll never, ever, forget that it was wrong, but how many times can I say that I'm sorry? How many times can I promise you that it *won't* happen again?" The tears were back. "For God's sake, Trevor, I was *drunk*; the vodka must have reacted with the anti-histamines I was taking. Okay, it's a poor excuse I know, but it happened and for that I'm truly sorry. For the hundredth time I'm sorry." Annabelle aimed her tear soaked face at Trevor.

Why? Why did it have to happen? He thrashed himself with the same old question. Okay – he reluctantly admitted to himself – the passion and the tenderness *had* gradually evaporated from their marriage; not helped by Jemma's birth six years ago. So perhaps he was as much to blame as his wife, but to have sex with another man…how could she have done such a thing?

"What if I'd done the dreaded deed? You know, gone and had it off with a bit of fresh. Come on then, Annabelle...tell me how you would have handled that scenario?"

"Perhaps I'd have smacked you, and scratched your eyes out. I might even have considered killing the filthy bitch who'd dropped her knickers for you." Tears made it difficult for her to look at her husband. "I don't know, Trevor. Damn it, I don't know." She sounded exhausted.

Their eyes locked and fought their own battle.

"I suppose you'd have preferred it if I'd broken my neck instead of your heart." More tears.

Raw emotions attacked Trevor. It felt like a python had coiled itself around his throat.

She used a tissue to dry her eyes. "You could *try* and forgive me. All I ask is that you try. I don't expect an immediate and full absolution for my sins." Her long fingers stroked the scar on her forehead.

Trevor's suffering reached new heights; his insides writhed in agony. That's it, he decided, enough is enough. The constant bickering and the hateful looks were destroying the whole family. It was time to make a new start.

He remembered that first meeting at the youth club at Burston Road High School. They were so young and innocent. He was fifteen, Annabelle a year younger. Starting off as friends, they both had a passion for reading. She liked Shakespeare, he preferred Dickens. Annabelle likened themselves to Romeo and Juliet. Trevor insisted they were more like David Copperfield and Dora. They not so much fell, as grew into love. Gradually, but nonetheless deeply, as their fictional counterparts.

Trevor wanted that special closeness back. He'd happily settle for a small portion of the intimacy they'd once shared. More than anything else, he wanted his best friend back.

He placed a hand on her shoulder. It was the first time he'd touched her since-

"I haven't seen you using the neck brace lately." He tried to sound interested in her progress.

"No, I was lucky; the whiplash wasn't as bad as it could have been. Nigel's side of the car took most of the impact.

Thank God we only hit a *small* tree." She tried to laugh.

"Bella."

"Y-e-s."

"How do you fancy coming with me to Whitby?"

Without wavering, she threw her arms around his neck.

The first kiss was wet and salty, but it felt so wonderful. Their tears comforted each other.

"Shout Jemma. Tell her to get dressed." Trevor felt alive again. "We're all going to the seaside. Fish and chips at the Magpie. How does that sound?" He resurrected the long lost smile. "Barkis is willin, Bella. Barkis is definitely willin."

Her face looked ten years younger. "Oh darling, thank you so much. As Willy Shakespeare rightly said, 'All's well that ends well'. The 'Bard' certainly knew a thing or two about love."

Whacker Spencer

"Mam, I feel sick. I'm not going to school today."

"That's a pity, John," Mam shouted upstairs. "Ya dad's put a rest day in, says he'll tek us all to Newark market. He said you and our Marlene could skip school. She's ever so excited. Ney mind son, you stay where ya are; I'll ask Mrs Waller to look in on you later on."

Mam's giggle echoed into my bedroom; she knew I was shamming. It was a Wednesday; I remember it well. I was fourteen and struggling with school and my education. My absenteeism record was dreadful.

I hated Wednesday's.

Correction…I hated Class 4A's last period on a Wednesday. The 3 o'clock to four Math's lesson with Whacker Spencer. Mister Spencer to his wizened old face. He took no prisoners, ruling with a rod of iron. To be more precise, a four-foot cane, thin and polished with the sweat of his victims palms. You could hear the swish from the back of the classroom. A wretched cry announcing its contact with the young and tender flesh.

Whacker was a tall man; his six foot height emphasised by a skeletal frame sculptured like a statue by his term of duty in The Kings Own Battalion. Ex Corporal Roderick Spencer was a widower. I well remember Dora, his wife of many years. She was a lovely woman. I was fortunate to have been taught by her in infant school. Short in the body with a homely more pretty face, she always had a smile on her face and was loved by all who met her. A dreadful illness forced her into early retirement. She didn't suffer for long – thank the Lord. The funeral service at St. Mark's overflowed with people paying their last respects. To this very day, the memory still brings a tear to my eyes.

But…more of Whacker. He picked on me. To be more precise, he singled me out and embarrassed me in front of my mates. You see, Maths was never my favourite subject. I just managed to hold my own with the times and division questions, but algebra and trigonometry blew my mind. In my teenager eyes, he knew this and played on my weakness. Asking me to go to the front of the class, he'd point his dreaded cane at the strange symbols and hieroglyphics scribbled on the blackboard.

"What does that mean?" He'd ask, staring over his horn rimmed spectacles into my vacant eyes.

What I didn't know until leaving school in the December of 1958, was that Whacker was in fact trying to help me.

I applied for my first job – an apprenticeship with a television shop. The interview went well. The owner manager – a Mr Shaw – asked if I could supply a written reference from my school headmaster, to confirm my grades and suitability for the job.

You've probably guessed…Whacker Spencer was also the headmaster, so I had grave misgivings about getting the job.

However…I needn't have worried.

Fully expecting to see a derisory appraisal from Whacker, I steamed open the letter. I couldn't believe what he had written.

Works hard. A good student. Will do well.

I got the job. I didn't stick it for long as the wages were crap. Dad got me a job at the pit. Better money.

<u>Yesterday, Today, and Tomorrow.</u>

"Put me sixpence each way on Dougie Smith in the 3 o'clock at Haydock Park."

I can hear Mum's words even now…forty years after she died. I must confess that I can't remember whether the horse won or not, but I mark the occasion as my first visit to the Turf Accountants – bookies to the non s porting readers who have mistakenly picked up this article thinking that it contained some prophetic guide lines as to their future.

Only fourteen at the time but big with it – as Dad always reminded me later in life – it was the same year that the Gent family went to Skegness and nearly lost their youngest member.

Our Geoff – only three and a bit years old – was fascinated with the little brown donkey with white ears that had just taken him on a magical tour of the golden sands. Before we knew it, the little bugger had vanished – my brother that is, not the donkey. I got the blame of course. 'You should have been watching him', Mum said through her tears.

To tell you the truth, I was much too busy watching Maureen Smith parading around in her bikini…I fancied her rotten. Now you must remember that I am reminiscing about the fifties, 1957 to be precise, and 'fancying' a girl was a naive teenager's attempt at sounding 'grown up'.

On the last night of our week's holiday, she put my hand on her chest…I nearly died. 'I've got a headache', I spluttered and went scuttling back to our chalet. Mum said that I looked a bit flushed…she'd have fainted if she'd known what her eldest son had just been stroking.

Sorry, I'm losing the plot…Oh to be young again.

The gambling…I was telling you about my initiation into the

Sport of Kings. Well at the time it was illegal to place any bets off the racecourse, hence the need for back-street 'bookies'. Ernie West, Nobby to his friends, for reasons I never asked about, came to the rescue. He ran his business from this glorified office no bi gger than a bike shed, just around the corner from where we lived.

The door was spragged open with a large lump of coal. A small, chubby man wearing a trilby stood in front of a blackboard on the wall to my left. A taller, red-faced chap, sat behind a scruffy, brown veneered table directly in front of me.

"Hey, do you want to get me arrested?" He said with a grin almost as wide as the shed.

"It's only Jack and Vera's eldest." The 'trilby' man said, waving a piece of chalk in my direction. "Sixpence each way on Dougie Smith in the 3 o'clock...am I right?" He looked me straight in the eye.

"Hey, mind your own business." Mister West winked to his mate. "You're only the marker upper, I'm the bookie. Give us the money lad, then off with you; it's nearly time for PC Plod to do his rounds." They laughed.

I passed him the shilling and ran home.

Times have certainly changed; you are now actually encouraged to go into Betting Shops. They supply wall to wall flat-screen telly's full of information on the runners, riders, and betting for any race in this country and abroad. You can even get refreshments to sustain you whilst you wait for the results.

Mum would have loved this modern approach to gambling, but the sixpence each way has gone along with Dougie Smith.

What about tomorrow? Who can tell? But I do know this, I'll be there, putting my money on the horses.

Thanks Mum for the legacy.

YOUNG AHAB

"There she blows."

I looked to the source of the outcry, the crow's nest. Nathan Baxter pointed to an object hidden from my eyes.

Eager to catch sight of my first whale, I ran to the starboard gunnel. Nothing; we were too far away. Disappointment filled my soul.

"Nor-nor-west, Captain; half a league at the most." Nathan pointed the way.

Captain Jacob Enderby appeared at my side. No longer a young man, he placed both elbows on the gnarled oak railing – steadying his balance against the rolling sea.

A telescope appeared against Enderby's right eye – as if it had heard Nathan's words and had flung itself into position.

"Nor-nor-west it is. Heave to bos'n." The captain spun around and faced the gathered crew. "He's a big'n and no mistake. Make ready to lower the boats. We'll have him tied alongside before sunset."

I looked for Samuel Pollard, my drinking partner. This was his second voyage on The Pride of Nantucket; he'd tell me what to do.

"Move your carcass, skinny ribs, and follow my lead," Samuel bawled. "Time to earn your rations."

Careful not to get in anyone's way, I did as told, moved to the opposite side of the nearest longboat and attacked the ropes holding it to the deck. Inexperience outweighed by the nimbleness of my long, slim fingers, I finished at the same time as my mentor. Job done, my heart raced fit to burst. I stared at my friend and awaited the next order.

"Well, Ahab, this is it, man against a monster. I hope your God has time to be with us today." Samuel grinned at me.

"Don't mock the Lord," I answered…surprised at my bravado.

"You Quakers. Some say as you're all hot air and bibles. It's soon enough we'll see if you've got the guts and stamina to match your tongue. The sperm whale takes no notice of sermons, no m atter who's doing the preaching." Samuel mocked as he passed me a harpoon. "Here…place it alongside them others and be careful how you handle it…the sharp end is for the whale." He laughed.

Enderby stood before the crew. "Well men, forty-five days out of New Bedford and the quarry lies before us. Time now to forget the comforts of home…especially the wives and the children." He scanned our faces. "Be on your mettle, for today we challenge the king of the waves, and he's fighting for his life. The beast will be angry, powerful in his rage. Kneel with me now and pray for divine protection…or a quick and painless dispatch to Davey Jones's locker. Whatever the God of the High Seas decides."

In the silence of prayer, I thought back to the day we left port…more so the night before our departure.

The Spouter Inn was full to the rafters with sailors. Old tars greedily knocking back the rum like it was the last drop of liquor they'd ever swallow, whilst the young pretenders – most of them orphans like Samuel and myself – fooled around like a mawkish bunch of wenches, pushing, slapping and squealing, ignorant of the enormity of putting our names on the Pride of Nantucket's human manifest.

"We're closing on hi m fast, Captain." Nathan Baxter's raucous cry dragged me back from my daydreaming reminiscences.

"So be it. Lower the boats and put your backs into it, men. Let's show that floating lump of blubber who's the master." Enderby moved with a new vigour.

"Out of the way, lad. That be my boat you're getting a ready."

The scarred and blotchy-faced sailor with a bent nose and leather patch over his left eye brushed by me, almost knocking me off my feet.

"I've heard 'em call you Ahab. Be that your first or last name, young'n?"

His one good eye – bloodshot and twitching – scanned me from top to bottom. "It's the only one I've ever known. Anyway...one name was good enough for Moses."

"So be it, lad. Then I'll be calling you Ahab." A one-sided smile exposed his rotting teeth. "My folks named me Jedediah Croft...but I've answered to the name Jed ever since my father, Abraham Croft, shook hands with Davey Jones in the foulest white squall known in these here waters. Aye...that was a bad day for meself and me mother. She only lasted a short while after...twas the smallpox that took her. From the first week in the first month of the year of our Lord eighteen hundred and twenty, I was on me own, no older than the number of fingers on both me hands, with no relatives and a face full of misery."

I forced myself to look beyond this sailor's features – the good book preaches that all men are equal in the eyes of our Lord. "I'll be saying a prayer for you, Jed. We'll share a snifter of rum when you get back." I smiled at him. His good eye stopped twitching for a few seconds; he climbed into the boat.

Samuel pulled at my arm. "Don't you be getting too familiar with Jed Croft. If you end up the wrong side of that fellow, he'll skin you alive."

I helped to lower Jed's boat. A clammy sweat encased my body – partly a result of my exertions...partly from the thought of Jed Croft taking a knife to my flesh.

Watching the line of boats draw away from The Pride of Nantucket, I wondered how long it would be before I had the chance to prove my worth as a harpooner.

"Watch and learn, Ahab." Samuel's words penetrated my thoughts. "And learn ye well, for the sea is a cruel teacher. One mistake is one too many with the likes of that big lump of blubber we be after killing this day."

*****

"Tie him up good; we'll slice him up in the morning." Captain Enderby took a couple of pulls on his pipe before turning his attention to me. "Ahab, get ya'self down the ladder and give Jed Croft a helping hand."

I jumped to attention. "Aye, aye, Captain." I was glad to be involved in the action but wary of displeasing the one-eyed sailor.

"Do as I tell ye lad…no more…no less, and we'll be done in no time at all; then we'll have a good long swallow o' rum." Something close to a smile exposed Jed's motley collection of teeth. "First job is to tidy up the boat. We can't have any tackle under our feet when we be squaring up to the likes of that big fella." He nodded to his latest victory then began to coil up a tangle of rope.

"How does it feel, Jed…you know…when you see your first harpoon sink into the whale's body?" I moved a bloodied harpoon to one side.

"Well enough lad…well enough. I be used to it by now, this being my fifteenth year before the mast; the last five of 'em with Captain Enderby."

Harpoons cleaned, ropes coiled and stashed away, I took a long look at the whale; this was the first real one I'd seen. Oh yes, I'd seen many a painting on the walls of alehouses, but in no way was I prepared for the sheer size of the whale. Half as long again as the boat, I could have pushed my fist into its blowhole.

"Mark ye well where the harpoons hit him. Aim for his eyes.

110

The blubber be thinner there. Two or three in there will finish him off. I've never heard of any of em needing a fourth."

Jed pointed to the three massive rips just behind the whale's eye. I couldn't believe how small the eye was in such an imposing beast.

"I have." A familiar voice said. "He's a body as white as a ghost, and they call him Moby-Dick."

It was Enderby, leaning over the railings, smoke billowing from his pipe.

"That be but a drunk's tale. Told out of one glass too many." Jed's eye stopped twitching.

"Maybe so, but I aim to find out. And it could be soon. I'm told that but a three day's sail will put us in the very waters of this 'super whale'."

The Captain locked eyes with me. "What say you, young'n? Are you ready for such an adventure?"

"Aye-aye, Captain."

"New Bedford's ship owners are keen to catch the likes of Moby-Dick. A whale that size will fill many a barrel of oil. Captain Machin of the Sea Urchin, be bragging in The Spouter Inn that his owners have gone and signed up a harpooner of the highest merit. He be costing them a small fortune. A ninetieth lay of the profits if truth be told. He be known by the name of Queequeg."

"That be a strange name," I raised an eyebrow.

"No stranger than the man." Jed gripped my arm.

"They're wasting their money, Captain. For Moby-Dick is ours." Filled with exuberance, the words jumped off my tongue. I closed my hand around the nearest harpoon.

Invisible fingers, cold and powerful, squeezed my heart as the words of the 23rd Psalm flooded my brain, 'I will fear no evil: For Thou art with me'.

Observations from a Sunlounger

"Ugh, it's hotter in Sheffield than it is here. We could have saved ourselves a fortune by staying at home."

"Will you stop your moaning and put some sun cream on my back. And wash your hands first; they're covered in ink from that newspaper you're been reading for the last hour. We come on holiday to relax, not to keep up to date with the doom and gloom of the world."

Putting The Sunday Mirror on the floor, Derrick heaved his body off the sunlounger. "It's about time they had some new mattresses; this one looks like an elephant has been sat on it."

Iris didn't say a word…just continued reading her book.

"Do you want a drink whilst I'm up?"

"Yes please; I'll have a coffee. No sugar; I'm watching my weight." She rubbed her tummy.

Hands washed, Derrick returned with the drinks.

"Guten Morgen."

"The same to you." Derrick responded to the swarthy looking chap the colour of a lobster wearing a pair of shorts louder than his voice.

"Who were you talking to?" She squinted under her Ray Ban's.

"I've no idea; never seen him before."

"He must have thought you were German; I told you to have a shave this morning."

"Shall I use the Piz Buin or the Ambre Solaire?" He offered both to his wife.

"I'll have the Ambre Solaire; it's a higher factor. I have to be careful the first few days of a holiday…I burn so easily."

"Good God woman. What's happened to your hair? It looks like a rats nest at the back."

"You do exaggerate. It's this hot weather and swimming in the sea; they play hell with my perm. But it's nice to know that you've noticed. Anything else you'd like to make comments about?"

"I can't remember this many lines on your neck last year."

"That's enough of the flattery; get back on your lounger." Iris gave him a look that would crack a brazil nut.

"I walked into Evie at the bar; we had a lovely chat."

"I bet you did."

"Yeah, she said they were hiring a car for a few days; her partner wanted to see more of the island. You met Evie and Roger at the Rep's meeting. You know…the man with a limp who reminded you of Hannibal Lecter."

"He gave me the creeps. He had this smarmy way about him; he never took his eyes off my chest."

"Perhaps he was admiring your necklace."

"The bulge in his trousers said otherwise. Such men should be castrated."

"That's a cruel thing to say; the poor man could be suffering with a hernia."

"Look, can we drop it? I'm here for a week's rest."

A silence descended.

"Hey…Look over there…He's smoking. I'm sure this is a non-smoking area." Derrick pointed at the little man with a cigar in his mouth.

"You're wrong you know; that's a designated area; can't you see it's surrounded by ashtrays?" Iris closed her book.

"Foreigners. They've no respect for other people."

"Let's go for a swim; it might cool you down." She put her Ray Bans in her handbag and led the way to the pool.

The little man with the cigar waved his paper at Derrick. "I say, Mate, how about doing a swop? Your Mirror for my News of the World."

Friendship

We go through life, our separate ways
Take different paths; meet varied fates
But loads seem lighter, and pain seems less
If by our sides, we have our mates

They say it's not, within our power
To choose our kin, our flesh and blood
But ours it is, by own free will
The choice of friends, for bad or good

They may be stubborn, weak or sick
They may be poor, or even smell
But when time it comes, to face the worst
They stand by us, through fire and hell

The flesh will heal; the bruise will go
The broken bones, will mend
But nought can ease, the pangs you feel
When you have lost, a trusted friend

I Wish, I Wish

I wish I could be happy and normal again
Free from anxiety, terrors, and fears
And walk to the shop, or just watch TV
Without feeling so low, close to tears

The black cloud of doom, is always around
From when I get up, till I sleep
I busy myself, doing tasks, big and small
That helps me my sanity, to keep

I'm told by the experts, the feelings I get
Are not real, but just in my head
Well all I can say, is when they get bad
I think I'd be better off dead

I feel like my throat, is going to close
And a lump is there most the time
So when I try, and swallow, I can't
Then I panic, and walls, I could climb

Globus Hystericus, my doctor assures me
Is what I am suffering from
Tension and stress, is the cause, so he says
So I shouldn't be frightened, or glum

I can either take tablets, or try therapy
But there's a six-month wait, for a place
In the meantime, I must, exist day to day
And my demons, and nightmares, must face

The Passing

There was a time not long ago
When I was content with my life
Although not rich in worldly ways
I knew little of troubles and strife

But then one day my partner said
She was feeling so tired and weak
And after waiting, too long, of course
Some medical help she did seek

The tests were made, results declared
The prognosis was hard to face
But being the person we knew that she was
She took it with calmness, and grace

Her life had been hard, but good, she said
She was taught to be grateful, and humble
For God decided on her fate
And who was she to grumble

Her time grew near, her body suffered
But her beliefs dulled all of the pain
For she was sure that when she passed
She'd see all of her loved ones, again

Now she has gone, I miss her so
But death as lost all of it's sting
For I know she's but a thought away
Carried to me, on Angels wing

We Must Forgive

We must forgive, the evil ones, who kill without a thought
And those who kick, and hurt us, and treat us like we're nought
We must forgive, who do us wrong, in any shape or form
For they are just the same as us, but their souls are cold not warm

We must forgive, the selfish deeds, of men who do not think
They have to have things all their way, or else they cause a stink
We must forgive, the hard and cruel, who show no signs of love
For they must suffer deep inside, and need help, from up above

We must forgive, our friends, who sometimes let us down
They may forget to phone us, then we sulk, and wear a frown
We must forgive, the nameless ones, in the papers every day
The media say they're guilty, for their sins, they have to pay

We must forgive, the terrorists, who act like they are God
No one is safe or innocent, they kill, at just a nod
If we can show true mercy, and accept, all flesh is weak
One day we may forgive ourselves, find the peace, that we all seek

Talk to God

When daily problems seem all too much
And you feel sad or out of touch
Don't shake your head, or start to frown
Just breathe in deep, look up, not down
Talk to God

When friends have dropped you like a stone
And you feel like you stand alone
Don't be upset, and full of fright
Just think of God, tell him your plight
Talk to God

We are not perfect; we sometimes sin
Then we feel shame, and bad, within
We think the future, we cannot face
And that we fail, the human race
Talk to God

In times of suffering and ill health
We curse our lack, of physical wealth
And blame it all, on Him above
And think that we, are short of love
Talk to God

For He is with you, night and day
All you have to do, is pray
Just tell Him what, is troubling you
And ask His help, to get you through
Talk to God

If I Fall Behind

I walk the path set out for me
The step in front is all I see
Each twist and turn, each hurdle met
I learn a bit, and stronger get

Sometimes I find my progress slow
And do not know which way to go
I weigh things up, inside my head
Then make my choice, and onward tread

But oft is wrong this road I take
And then I learn by my mistake
If once you've failed, success is sweet
So do not frown, if tests you meet

The tears I shed when I feel pain
Will grow my soul, like seeds in rain
And hardships met, and tossed aside
I know will help, me storms to ride

Our health and wealth we do not choose
Sometimes we win, but oft we lose
But if we face, each day with hope
I know we'll have, the strength to cope

Many are the trials we'll meet
Before we're ready, our Lord to greet
So onward go, take faith with thee
If I fall behind, please wait for me

My Rainbow

What colour is the truth Lord?
I think it's white as snow
And amethyst is hope Lord
Without it we cannot grow

I'm pretty sure tranquillity
Is a gorgeous shade of blue
And red for strength and courage
That keeps us straight and true

The vivid green, I see as growth
And yellow means warmth and light
The palest pink means innocence
And knowing that you are right

I know for sure that sombre black
Is the colour of despair
And silver is the sign of calm
So elusive and so rare

And last but the most precious
Is the purest deepest gold
The love you blindly give us
As promised in days of old

My rainbow means so much to me
The colours never lie
Sometimes they lift my Spirits high
But oft they make me cry

A Christmas to Remember

The Lord decided in his wisdom, 'twas time for us to change
He'd watched us with our easy lives; thought time to rearrange
He waited till the Christmas Eve, quite good of him I thought
Before he blessed the both of us, with a present that he bought

It wasn't what we asked for, but we got it just the same
My wife fell down our daughter's stairs, with only fate to blame
She broke her leg, was in a mess, the pain was hard to bear
She went into the hospital, for a plaster cast to wear

We take for granted, most of us, that we can walk or run
But when you are disabled, life is hard, and not much fun
A stick or crutch is needed now, to help in getting round
And cleaning up and cooking, too much for her, she found

'Twas now my skills in domesticity, were put to the acid test
Competent in many tasks, my cooking was poor, at best
My wife is on the mend at last, she's sick of beans on toast
She says she wants her kitchen back, and needs a Sunday roast

Although we did not get the gifts, we expected Christmas Day
The lessons that God taught us, are with us, night and day
We look at life so different now, be a friend, to the weak and slow
For as we help less fortunate ones, our spiritual side, will grow

Help Us

Lord I ask for you to help us
To guide and show the way
I know that life is but a rehearsal
And mankind should get wiser each day

But sometimes when I look around
And see all the evil and greed
It's hard for me to understand
When you say 'Love, is all you need'

Your teachings say 'Be kind to all'
And wealth and position mean naught
But today's society, is hungry for power
So wars of possession are fought

Please send out your guardian angels
To enter our souls when we sleep
And pass on your doctrine of love
Then hopefully no more will we weep

For love is surely the answer
It's impartial to colour and tongue
Worth more than all treasures or chattels
Yet is free to the weak, or the strong

To receive love you first have to give it
Without question or limits or cost
And with heavenly help from our father
Then humanity will never be lost

Grace

Love is the cure for all of our ills
God gives it freely; it's better than pills
Hope keeps us going when all seems bleak
Faith gives the answers, to questions we seek

What more can we ask, from Heaven above
If we have faith, hope and love
All else is material, and comes and goes
Today we are rich, tomorrow who knows

Peace of mind and a happy soul
Surely must be, our ultimate goal
And we must make, each stranger a friend
Then wars and hostilities will end

For we are all children of God
Following the path, that he once trod
Some steps are easy and others so hard
But strength and character will be our reward

We all take for granted this Earth of ours
The streams, the forests, the flowers
The fruits of the land, the Sun, and the rain
All life in the sea, the air and the plain

God has allowed us to use them awhile
But they are just borrowed, merely on trial
For when we have moved, to the higher sphere
Our children will inherit, what we leave, here

A Thought Away

We all have worries and aches and pains
It seems our bodies are trapped in chains
Now close your eyes, your torments release
A thought away, is hope and peace

Just let your spirit fly high above
Don't think of hate, think only of love
Imagine that you're bathed in light
And angels are singing, dressed in white

No signs of mans destruction or greed
All shackles removed, our true self freed
We float amidst, the vistas of beauty
Time is forgotten, so is fear, and duty

The colours around us are vivid and bright
Nothing is hidden, away from our sight
We see only truth, feel happy and calm
All illnesses smothered, in God's healing balm

Our loved ones and friends now gather around
Lost to us once, but all are now found
When all is revealed, our fears will cease
A thought away, is hope and peace

A Prayer for Today

God give me the peace and comfort
I remember when I was a lad
When pains and troubles entered my life
I just called for my Mum, or my Dad

Most troubles then were oh so simple
And were quickly dispatched with much love
And if sometimes that wasn't enough
We would ask for some help, from above

But sadly today our values have changed
We run to and fro with great haste
The clock is ever our master now
And patience and calm, deemed a waste

We do not have time for anything now
We are too busy grabbing for all
The media news is all doom and gloom
They rejoice, showing somebody fall

I ask you Lord to please use your power
To slow down your children gone mad
We all forget we are here to learn
And that sinning, and hatred, are bad

We are surely on the path to destruction
When compassion and love count for naught
But if this is the price we must pay
I think progress has been too dearly bought

Let's return to our old fashioned thinking
That 'tis better to give than receive
And with God's love and wisdom to guide us
No more will we hurt, or deceive

Into the Silence

We bow our heads in worship
And pray to God above
We ask forgiveness for our sins
For he is full of love

And as we go into the silence
We feel the peace and calm
Our spirit guides and loved ones
Will protect us from all harm

All pains and troubles leave us now
And we are blessed to see
Ourselves for what we really are
Not as we seem to be

The veils of lies all melt away,
The truth is known at last
For now the fears and doubts we had
Are dimly in the past

All doors are open to us now,
We travel where we will
We meet old friends and loved ones
Who say they're with us still

And if we need their help sometimes
Or just to guide our way
They say they never left us
They are just a thought away

We ask God for some healing,
To help the sick we know
For he is all around us,
And the angels watch us grow

Locks and Keys

We enter into this World alone
Our life a clean new slate
We do not know of fear or sorrow
Or how to love or hate

As we grow in body and mind
We'll walk the path our parents trod
And if we're lucky and stay on track
We'll learn of truth, of love, and God

We wonder what life's secrets are
Why we are here, what is in store
Will we be happy, or very sad
Will we be rich, or maybe poor

Some answers we seek are easy to find
And right and wrong always known
For deep inside our very essence
Is the seed of wisdom God has sown

If we but knew that round the bend
Just out of reach almost in sight
Where all the answers that we seek
Content we'd be, our worries slight

If we learn to trust our inner thoughts
And listen to the Spirit voice
Then what is right and best for us
Will become so clear, the only choice

For every lock there is a key
It may be lost, or hard to find
But if we trust in God above
He'll put the keys inside our mind

<u>Miss Evelyn Carrington</u>

I walked into our church today
To hear a speaker new to me
She looked quite old and very grey
Not what I thought Id see

For I had heard how good she was
And a legend of our time
They said she served the church so well
And was surely in her prime

After she opened with a prayer
She told us some philosophy
About how times are getting hard
But we are blessed and free

For we are members of a faith
That is spiritual and true
And we all know our angel friends
Are around us, me and you

As she spoke, and moved around
It soon became quite clear
That she had surely got the gift
And her spirit guides were near

The messages that she received
From our friends and loved ones gone
Were taken with uplifted hearts
As we acknowledged every one

She closed with thoughts of love and hope
And told us, "do your best"
We thanked her for inspiring us
And for leaving us so blessed

Music

Our World Is Full Of Music
So Pleasing to Our Ears
It Soothes Our Ragged Nerves
Helps To Allay Our Fears

The Gurgling Of The Brook
As It Slowly Passes Bye
The Robins Cheerful Song
The Sparrows Chirpy Cry

The Rustling leaves Of Autumn
As They Dance And Swirl Around
The Pitter Pat Of Rainfall
As It Falls On Stony Ground

A Baby's Gurgling Answer
To Mothers Hugs, And Kisses
Our Loved Ones Voices Saying
'Many Birthday Wishes'

The Cockerel's Rousing Chorus
At The Opening Of The Day
The Laughter Of The Children
As They Run Around And Play

For This We Must Be Thankful
To Our Lord On High Above
For He Doth Wrap These Wondrous Sounds
In Parcels Of His Love

Stand By Me

I ask you Lord to stand by me
To help me through my darkest hour
I feel so low and all alone
Please hold my hand, give me your power

I question not why I am ill
For I know you have marked my way
But I am human, and feel the pain
And get weaker each passing day

Just give me strength to carry on
To keep my dignity unto the last
I do not want to be a burden
Support me now as in the past

And when it's time for my transition
Don't let me pass in fear or hate
Then all my loved ones I leave behind
Will peacefully accept my fate

The Answer is Within

These times we live in are troubled, we live at such a pace
Mankind is taught to push and grab, what's become of the human race
You may find that your suffering, from troubles old and new
And that your times of happiness, are far between and few

It may seem that we are better off, than our parents used to be
But consumer goods and motor cars, I'd swap for a heart that's free
Today we can't have just a cold, or a simple stomach bug
Instead we all have heart attacks, feel the need for pill and drug

We all ask why our lives are tough, why lessons are hard to learn
The reason should be obvious, our contentment we have to earn
It's only with our facing strife, that we can prove our worth
And hopefully we'll help and love, as we journey on this earth

So try to be the best you can, greet strangers with a smile
Don't be afraid to say you're wrong, be forgiving all the while
When in distress just turn to God, make your peace and then begin
Tell Him what hurts or worries you, he'll say the answer is within

The Path

He puts us on the path of life
And guides us on our way
We make mistakes and sin a lot
As we progress day by day

He knows that in this mortal coil
Our values are selfish and vain
We do not think of others needs
Just what we have to gain

But as we slowly travel onward
We start to know what's right
That truth and love and kindness
Are worth more than gold and might

Some of us have many trials
The future is often bleak
We cry out Lord please help us
For the flesh is oh so weak

Then God sends out his angels
To be near us in our need
It does not matter if we're poor
Nor what our race or creed

Although we may not see them
We feel their healing balm
All pains and terrors leave us
We are protected from all harm

When he thinks we have proved ourselves
And nothing else to give
He guides us o'er the ethereal bridge
Then in the Summerland we'll live

The Shopping List

I've just made out a shopping list
And I'm sending it to God
I'm asking for the things we need
On this Earth where his son once trod

Strength and Courage would help indeed
And Peace and Quiet is a must
Kindness Truth and Honesty
And a bucketful of Trust

A little bit of Hope and Faith
With some Patience to wash it down
A large amount of Wisdom
And some Joy in case we frown

Health and Happiness a lot
And a bunch of Humility
Atop the list is Love of course
Then we'll live in Harmony

He Wipes The Slate Clean

I say some things I do not mean
They can be hurtful and unkind
I then feel bad and hate myself
I'll make amends, forgiveness find

My thoughts are oft selfish it's true
I only think what pleases me
But I wouldst ask another chance
To see your point, share pain with thee

I only see the things I want
And I'm blind selectively
Like many of the human race
I expect to be fed and free

Some things I've done I do regret
The sins of flesh tempt me
But now I see where I went wrong
Forgive my weakness, I do plea

I look upon my life so far
As my first day in infant school
And errors made on my blackboard
God will erase at my renewal

They say that time awaits no man
Tides ebb and flow each day
But sins and fears are not forever
All you have to do is pray

Wouldst

If thou wouldst dwell at God's right side
Be calm of self, with love your guide
Do not get lost, or lose your way
Believe yourself, just kneel and pray

It matters nought, what others think
You know the truth, you're on the brink
You have the faith, the cause is just
Your time is now, in God you trust

Stand by your dreams of better things
You think you're small but you're spirit has wings
Wouldst give the heart, wouldst give the soul
What once was part, is now the whole

Transition

Take my hand for I am going
To a place I have never been
I do not know the way at all
But I hope it's warm and green

I'm not sure of the distance
Or how I will get there
So as I've done these many times
I ask for help, inside a prayer

Forgive me if I hesitate
Or if I start to cry
I'll find it hard to just let go
But I promise I will try

I've heard that at transition
All fear and pains will end
And then we're led into the light
By the angels that you send

I only ask of you my God
That you will stand by me
I'm weak and only human
Please help me to break free

And if you've time to do it
I ask with all my heart
Please let my friends and loved ones know
'Tis not the end but my new start

Tomorrow

Tomorrow is another day
But now it seems so far away
I feel coiled up just like a spring
My nerves stretched taut, ready to ping

I try to see a ray of hope
As I slide down my slippery slope
But what's the good of life eternal
If your quality of life's infernal

I know that some are worse than me
And for their courage I do plea
But when you fight for your next breath
You feel so very close to death

It's not the passing that I fear
For I know God is standing near
But being human I do not know
How bad the pain and fear will grow

So everytime my health gets worse
I try to pray instead of curse
And ask the Lord why I should stay
Tomorrow is another day

The Stairway

I'm searching for the answers, and I'm looking high and low
To questions I am asking, on how we live and grow
I've asked my elders and the wise
I seek the truth, the facts, not lies

It's easy to delude ourselves, as many of us do
About what happens to us, when our life on earth is through
Some say at death we just expire
And then descend to Hell's cruel fire

But I believe, at end of day
When we must pass, for we can't stay
We leave behind the bone and skin
That hid the jewel, our soul within

Untethered now we float on air
Until we reach the gates most fair
They're made of pearls and open wide
And all that come are let inside

We find that now we're in a hall
All marbled floors and ceilings tall
And rising up as clear as day
Can only be Heaven's Stairway?

With hope we stand on bottom stair
What lies ahead we're not aware
The next step taken is on trust
So strength and courage is a must

And as we climb we start to find
We've left all pains and fears behind
It's now we're filled with faith and love
For God awaits us, up above

The First Stone

It's easy to be critical
And call someone a fool
Or play the game of Tit for Tat
Be horrible and cruel

But all of us should ponder
On who and what we are
And ask ourselves the question
Are we truly up to par?

For who of us as never
Told lies to save our face
And pushed and tugged the innocent
For intruding in our space

I know I'm far from perfect
And selfish to the core
For when I know I've got enough
I grab and take some more

To lust and crave and covet
Be it flesh or power or wealth
Is just as bad and odious
If achieved with grace or stealth

So let us all admit our faults
As we sit atop our throne
And he who's pure and free from sin
Let him cast the first stone

The Christmas Gift

The time of year is round again
The season to rejoice
For Jesus Christ was born this day
And a manger was his choice

To mark the coming of our Lord
Mankind will celebrate
We'll sing the songs of Christmas
Give thanks and venerate

We'll eat and drink the festive fare
As if there's no tomorrow
And as we cheer and raise a toast
We'll banish pain and sorrow

The shops are full of wondrous things
To tempt us at this time
The choice is wide and wonderful
From the mundane to the sublime

And as we wrap our presents
To give to ones we love
Remember as you do it
Give thanks to Him above

Number One

When I was but in infant school, I always did my best
I'd use my chalks and crayons, be a good boy not a pest
When time it came to decide, who would have the honoured task
Of giving out the daily milk, my teacher did others ask

When Big School I did attend, to climb the ladder was my aim
I did my lessons and homework, behaved, and played the game
A prefect's post I did attain, and hoped for better things
I got the job of Vice Captain, second place, again it stings

I fell in love, surprised myself, with a beauty from our street
My heart would lift into my mouth, when with a kiss we'd greet
It seemed so perfect and sublime, but Paradise came to an end
She said goodbye and went away, in the arms of my best friend

I put my pen to paper, my heartbreak did I trace
I sent it to the Writers Guild, my prize was second place
I know I'm less than perfect, and my hair and teeth have gone
I'll never play for England, but with God I'm Number one

Last Night

I thought I heard a voice last night, as I settled down to sleep
It sounded like my mother. I sat up, and I did weep
The reason for the flow of tears, is my mother's dead and gone
She passed away too suddenly, and it's dark where once she shone

I never got the chance to tell, how much I loved her so
I used to tell her in my head, and I thought that she would know
It's many years since we lost her, but I think of her each day
I ask God to be good to her, when I kneel me down to pray

Jesus wants me for a sunbeam, was her favourite song of praise
And everytime she heard it, her spirits it would raise
I must confess I took it bad, when she left us all so quick
I could not grieve as others did, I felt empty, sad, and sick

One day I began to know, twas time to show my love
I cried and cried for hours, asked for help from up above
I now believe in eternal life, that the soul goes on and on
For last night my Mum did call, to prove she hasn't gone

I Want To...

I want to live a happy life
And by God's grace, know little strife
I want to see the end of war
The end of greed, and no one poor

I want to see the children smile
As they run around and play awhile
And in their face no sign of sorrow
Let them know joy and a bright tomorrow

I want to walk and take the air
At my own pace, without a care
And not be chased by man or time
Where peace abounds and noise a crime

I want to feel content inside
And know at least that I have tried
I hope that as I've passed their way
I've put some joy in someone's day

I want to give more than I take
And mend more hearts than I do break
Return all kindness I've been shown
By friends and strangers I have known

I want to go to bed at night
And know I've done less wrong than right
Then when I lay me down to sleep
My soul will smile, instead of weep

I want to know that when I'm gone
I'm missed by some and cursed by none
Then when I'm met by God above
He'll say I've lived my life with love

I Choose

I choose to be the best I can
And try to love my fellow man
He may not have my thoughts or views
But he has toiled and paid his dues

I choose to listen with my heart
I know it is the way to start
I'll truly try to understand
And offer out, my welcome hand

I choose to see the truth in all
And listen not to those who call
For those who smear behind your back
Are false, and moral fibre lack

I choose to have a happy smile
Forget all troubles for a while
I won't be sad and sorry feel
I'll talk to God, and he will heal

I choose to be an open ear
Help those who live in mortal fear
For great's the pain of troubled mind
They with my help, some peace may find

I choose to live The Christian Way
Attend the church and to God pray
And know I well that win or lose
I went my way, and I did choose

Be Still

Turn your thoughts of fear inward
Be Still
Think only of peace
Be Still
Feel the storms in your head calm
Know that you'll come to no harm
With each breath that you take
Be Still

Put your faith in the Lord
Be Still
For He stands by your side
Be Still
You will never alone be
For He's watching o'er thee
And His love is eternal
Be Still

<u>Ode to the Invisible Man</u>

What can you do when it's never enough?
What can you say when nobody listens?
You can only give all that you possess
Why do others get smooth, and you only rough?

It's painful and sad to be put in second place
And agony when your lower in favour
I honestly think you should earn your respect
And not be ignored or slapped in the face

Enough is enough, you can take it so long
But when last straw is placed on Camel's back
No matter how strong, it crumbles and breaks
Then what once was, is not, and sad is the song

Tears will be shed and harsh words spoken
Lives will be changed not always for better
The future for all, will be tainted and strange
When the Invisible Man's heart, is finally broken

Great Expectations

I was born into the Working Class
In December forty-three
My father was a miner
He gave his name to me

My mother was the youngest of ten
And knew what hardship meant
She lost her dad when she was young
He left them without a cent

My parents told a tale so sad
Of how it was hard to survive
To keep a roof over our head
And feed and clothe us five

They did their best, they scrimped and saved
And sacrificed so much
To raise me and my sister and brother
All with their loving touch

I once asked Dad, and also me Mam
If they wished they'd been born today
And brought up with more worldly wealth
More time to sit and play

To my surprise, they both said no
They would not have changed their lot
For they'd had nowt, and managed well
Whilst we have all, but lost the plot

MATINS

LORD GUIDE US THROUGH THIS DAY
PROTECT US FROM ABOVE
SHOW US THE WAY TO LIGHT AND TRUTH
ENFOLD US WITH YOUR LOVE

VESPERS

LORD GUARD US THROUGH THIS NIGHT
PLEASE BANISH ALL OUR FEARS
LET ANGELS BE OUR COMPANY
TILL LIGHT OF MORN APPEARS